D0832483

GO FOR THE GLORY

GOLDEN FILLY SERIES

GO FOR THE
GLORY

LAURAINE SNELLING

BETHANY HOUSE PUBLISHERS
MINNEAPOLIS, MINNESOTA 55438

Horse on cover courtesy of Eagle Creek Stables, Inc.,
Shakopee, Minnesota.
Scene for cover courtesy of Four Footed Fotos,
Issaquah, Washington.

Cover illustration by Brett Longley,
Bethany House Publishers staff artist.

Copyright © 1991
Lauraine Snelling
All Rights Reserved

Published by Bethany House Publishers
A Ministry of Bethany Fellowship, Inc.
6820 Auto Club Road, Minneapolis, Minnesota 55438

Printed in the United States of America

Library of Congress Cataloging-in-Publication Data

Snelling, Lauraine.
    Go for the glory / Lauraine Snelling.
       p.   cm. — (Golden filly series ; bk. 3)
    Summary: After a string of wins, Trish breaks her arm, and since
the horse Trish and her father have entered in both the Santa Anita
Derby and the Kentucky Derby won't tolerate another rider, it seems
that they're going to miss the greatest opportunity of their lives.

    [1. Horse racing—Fiction. 2. Christian life—Fiction.]
I. Title. II. Series: Snelling, Lauraine. Golden filly series ; bk. 3.
PZ7.S677Go   1991
[Fic]—dc20   91–4126
                                            CIP
ISBN 1–55661–218–4   AC

To my son Brian,

my friend.

LAURAINE SNELLING is a full-time writer who has authored several published books, sold articles for a wide range of magazines, and written weekly features in local newspapers. She also teaches writing courses and trains people in speaking skills. She and her husband Wayne have two grown children and make their home in California.

Her life-long love of horses began at age five with a pony named Polly and continued with Silver, Kit, Rowdy, and her daughter's horse Cimeron, who starred in her first children's book *Tragedy on the Toutle*.

CHAPTER 1

Icy rain trickled down her neck. Tricia Evanston, sixteen-year-old wonder jockey at Oregon's Portland Meadows racetrack, crouched higher over her mount's withers. "Come on, girl," she sang to the filly's twitching ears. "Let's do this one. You know we like winning."

The dark bay filly settled deeper on her haunches. Firefly's ears pricked forward, nearly touching at the tips. She not only liked winning, she acted as if all the spectators came just to watch her. Besides loving to run, she was a natural performer.

The horse next to them refused to enter the starting gate. The memory of slashing whips flitted through Trish's mind. But the jockey who'd caused those accidents had been barred from the track.

Trish sniffed. In the cold, her nose ran nearly as fast as the horses. "Come on, get him in," she muttered.

The rear gates slammed shut. Trish and Firefly both tensed for the shot. The front gates clanged open. The filly burst from the stall, her haunches thrusting them ahead of the horse on their left. Three powerful strides and they had the rail.

Trish kept a firm hold on the reins. Pouring rain meant a slippery track, no matter how much sand the crew worked into the dirt. The marker poles flashed past.

By the six-furlong post, Firefly was running easily in the lead. She never seemed to care if the track was muddy or dry. She ran for the pure joy of it. Trish loosened the reins and let the filly have her head. She won by a furlong and was still picking up speed at the wire.

Trish laughed as she pulled her mount down and turned back to the grandstand. "You're fantastic!" She stroked the filly's wet neck, then rose in the stirrups for the slow gallop back to where her brother David and father Hal waited in the winner's circle. "Shame there wasn't a bigger crowd for you to dance for," she teased her horse. "Too many people stay home when it rains."

Trish glanced up at the glass-fronted grandstand. The sheeting rain made everything look dreary. But with a win like she'd had, it was as if the sun shone brightly.

Trish slid to the ground and unhooked her saddle, almost in the same motion. Firefly posed for the camera. David thumped Trish on the arm and her father gave her a quick hug.

"We should take Firefly with us to Santa Anita," Trish said, grinning at her father. "She needs a bigger crowd."

Hal nodded as he stroked the filly's nose. "She sure struts her stuff. And she's not even tired. What'd you do, just take her out for a Saturday stroll?"

Trish laughed again as she stepped on the scale. "She was still picking up speed at the wire. I couldn't believe it. David, you better give her a treat; she earned it."

"Yes, ma'am." David touched the rim of his hat in a mock bow. "You mind if we get out of the rain now?"

Trish returned his arm thump. "At least you've got a dry stall to work in." She looked skyward. "I've three more mounts—in this."

"Nobody said life was easy, or dry." David tugged on

the filly's reins. "Come on, horse." He stopped after they'd taken only a couple of steps. "You be careful, Tee. All those horses aren't mudders, like this one here."

"Yes, *Mother*."

David shook his head and trotted off to the testing barn with Firefly.

"He's right, you know." Hal fell into step beside his daughter.

"Da-ad."

"I'm not being over-protective, Tee. I've seen some pretty nasty spills on days like today. Just keep your guard up." He stopped at the entrance to the dressing rooms. "And Tee, that's not a bad idea."

Trish replayed his last comment in her mind as she entered the steamy room. She knew he'd been referring to her suggestion about Santa Anita. She and her father had that kind of mutual understanding. Sometimes it seemed they could almost read each other's mind.

Trish pulled her crimson-and-gold winter silks over her head. Her long-sleeved, insulated underwear top was wet around the neck but the waterproofed silks kept her body dry. She toweled the edges of her dark hair, and grabbing a brush out of her sports bag, gave it a good brushing. The longer length felt good.

Trish stared longingly at the steamy shower room where someone was singing as she soaped. A quick glance at her watch settled it. No hot shower. She put on the black and white diamond-patterned silks and headed out for her next ride. On her way out the door she applied a thick coating of lip balm and grabbed a handful of tissues to stuff up her sleeve. She would need them for her runny nose.

Rain blew over the track in sheets as they entered the

gates for the sixth race of the day, Trish's third. The race was for maidens under four, making it this colt's first race. And he didn't like the rain.

"Don't worry, fella, the rest of us don't like this any better than you do, so let's just get the job done." A horse two stalls over reared and backed out of the gate.

"Not now, you crazy thing." Trish kept her mutterings in the sing-song cadence that always soothed her mount. She tightened her shoulders up to her ears. *Man, it's cold*, she thought.

As the gates swung open, her mount slipped before regaining his footing. Trish kept his head up and let him gather himself together before urging him on. They were already two lengths behind the field.

Once he was running smoothly, she brought him up along the outside. They went into the far turn in fourth place with Trish encouraging him to reach for the leaders.

The horse on the rail slipped and bumped the one next to him. That horse went down, the rider flying over his mount's head.

Trish's horse skidded. He shied to the right. Trish caught herself, arms wrapped around his neck and nearly on his head.

The colt slipped again but veered around the jockey in the mud. Trish scrambled back in the saddle and yelled in his ears. "Now get on with it, we've still got a race to run."

The horse bobbled again but straightened out and crossed the wire with a show. "Third place is sure better than a fall," Trish consoled both him and herself as they cantered around to the winner's circle.

Her hands were still shaking when she stripped off

her saddle and stepped on the scale.

"Bad 'un out there," the steward said. "You handled him real well."

"Anyone hurt?" Trish shivered and ducked her chin in her collar.

"Not so's you'd notice. One good thing about the mud, it cushions a fall."

"Yeah, well thanks." *But that was awful close,* she thought. *Good thing Mom wasn't here to see that one.*

By the end of the day Trish was nearly frozen, and exhausted, but higher than the flagpoles standing at attention in the infield. Three wins on four mounts. And in weather like this. She ignored the shaking and hugged the happiness to herself as she trotted out to the car where her father waited for her. David and his best friend, Brad Williamson, who worked for their Runnin' On Farm, would load the horses in the trailer and meet them at home.

Hal snapped his seat upright when Trish turned her key in the lock. By using every moment to rest, he was able to keep up the restricted schedule the cancer treatments imposed on him. "Congratulations! You set yourself a record."

"I can hardly believe it." Trish tossed her sports bag in the backseat, then slid into the driver's seat. "And Firefly won a good purse, too. That should help the old checkbook."

"It will. You hungry?"

Trish shot him a tolerant look. When wasn't she hungry after a day of racing? "Are you?"

Hal nodded. "But you know Mom will have dinner ready."

Trish took a deep breath. She mentally finished his

thought. *And she'll be worrying about us, too.* "So we'll go to the drive-in window. I won't tell if you don't." The entire family had an unwritten pact. Anytime they could get food into Hal, they did. The chemotherapy killed his appetite along with the disease.

The rain had stopped by the time they crossed the I–5 bridge between Portland and Vancouver. Car lights reflected off the wet girders and shiny asphalt. Trish sipped her Diet Coke, the warmth of the car and the pleasure of her father's company mixed with the day's wins to create a perfect moment in time. She shot a "thank you" heavenward.

"I think we'll do it," Hal said, slurping his chocolate shake dry.

"Take Firefly?"

"Um-m hm-m. We'll check out the stakes book when we get home. The Santa Anita Oaks for fillies on Saturday would be a great race for her. Taking two won't be much more expensive than one."

"Does Bob Diego have room in his van for more than one?"

"Should have. I think he's taking just one horse."

Trish felt like hugging her father. Taking their colt Spitfire to the Santa Anita Derby in southern California was exciting enough, but riding three mounts at that track? *Wowee! What if all our horses win?* She corrected the if. *What'll we do when they all win?* Not only would the money be fantastic, but not very many women raced at that prestigious track. And few of those ever won.

She resolutely pushed aside thoughts of what her mother would have to say. Marge had been even more against her daughter riding since the incidents with the jockey striking their horses during several recent races.

Hal patted her knee, knowing her thoughts. "It'll be okay, Tee. I'll handle your mother."

Trish flashed him a grateful smile.

Surprisingly, Marge didn't have a lot to say, other than "congratulations" accompanied by a quick hug. She just shook her head when Hal mentioned taking Firefly along to Santa Anita. But her tight jawline revealed more of her true feelings.

Trish overheard her mother talking to her father when she passed their room on her way to the bathroom later that night.

"It doesn't matter what I think," Marge said. "You and Trish will do what you want to do anyway. You *know* how I feel. It's bad enough for her to race here, but California and then Kentucky scares me to death."

Trish shut her bedroom door. She didn't want to hear any more. Her mother's fears always managed to take some of the joy from her racing.

The next morning the Evanstons sat in their usual pew at church, right behind the Seaboldts. Rhonda winked over her shoulder at Trish. The two had been best friends since kindergarten.

When the pastor spoke about not being afraid, Trish wanted to nudge her mother. *How much easier life would be if Mother weren't such a worrier!*

Pastor Ron repeated the verse. "Be not afraid, for I am with you."

Trish's mind flitted back to the times her horses had been struck. By the third incident, she'd known what fear was. And anger. But it hadn't slowed her down any, in spite of Marge's anxiety.

Trish shook her head. Why couldn't her mother quit worrying?

She shuddered again when her father's name was said during the prayers for healing. Why did *everyone* have to know their business? Now people would ask about the chemotherapy and her father would tell them how things were going. It made her want to melt into a little puddle and seep into the ground. It was *so* embarrassing.

"I'll be over after lunch," Rhonda promised as they left the church. "Then you can tell me all about yesterday. Three wins. Awesome!"

"And you can quiz me for our history test. I *hate* memorizing dates."

"Both of you can muck out stalls in your spare time." David grinned as he interrupted them. "Keep you from getting bored."

"Right!" Rhonda and Trish laughed when they said the word at the same time.

That afternoon the weak sun split the clouds just above the western horizon as the girls headed down to the barns to visit Miss Tee, Trish's two-month-old filly.

She nickered at the sound of Trish's voice. While she still dashed behind her mother when strangers approached, she came forward when Trish called. Rhonda stood still and let the filly come to her. She extended the grain in the palm of her hand. The filly nibbled the oats, her soft nose whiskering Rhonda's palm. With a final lick not a trace remained.

Trish hugged her baby and scratched behind Miss Tee's tiny, pointed ears. The foal rubbed her head on Trish's chest.

"You are so-o-o lucky," Rhonda said. "She's about the prettiest thing around. And what a sweetie."

"I know. She's special all right. And she should be

fast. Look at Spitfire. Miss Tee's his full sister." Trish turned and stroked the mare. "You've done a good job, old girl." The mare shifted to rest the other back foot and leaned her head against Trish for more scratching.

After one last pat, Trish snapped a lead rope on the mare's halter and handed the shank to Rhonda. "Here, you lead her and I'll bring Miss Tee. She's not too happy yet when I lead her by herself. This way we'll fool her. Let's take the trail to the woods."

"Take your time, the work's all done anyway," David called as they trotted down the two-track dirt road.

"Thanks, we will." Rhonda grinned at Trish. "Has he always been so bossy?"

"He's gotten worse." Trish tugged on the lead rope. "Come on, Miss Tee. You need a run."

Half an hour later the girls came back up the rise with the horses. Trish was still puffing when she unsnapped the leads and put the mare and her foal back in their stall. She took a deep breath. "I'll get the feed if you'll fill the water bucket."

Rhonda's deep breath matched Trish's. "Boy, we need to do some running again. I can see weight training isn't enough."

"Yeah, and I haven't even had time for that lately."

"How come you had the afternoon off?"

"They scratched my two rides yesterday. One had shins and the other spiked a temperature. Maybe it's this yucky weather."

The weather became the topic of conversation at dinner that evening when Hal talked about their nomination for the Santa Anita Derby. At his mention of sunny California, Trish closed her eyes for a moment and tried to remember what warm sun felt like on bare skin.

"Maybe I can get a tan while we're down there."

Her mother's frown made Trish bite her lip.

"I'm sending in our nomination for the Kentucky Derby also," Hal said. "That $600 includes the rest of the triple crown too."

The Kentucky Derby! Trish ignored the thought of Belmont and the Preakness. It was like her dreams could only reach so far.

"Even if we don't get to go, better $600 now than $4,500 later."

"They sure up the fees when the race gets closer," Trish said, leaning on her elbows. "Doesn't seem fair."

"Since when did fair count?" Marge muttered as she rose from the table. She clattered the dishes into the sink and poured herself a cup of coffee. "Racing here is bad enough, but clear across the country? There are so many things that can go wrong. Driving over the mountains. Transporting a horse in an airplane. All the time Trish will miss from school. And how are we going to keep up with everything else around here? David isn't a super-man, you know."

"*Mom.*" David shook his head. "We'll do just fine. They'll be going to California over spring break and we just won't race any of our horses then. By the time they leave for Kentucky, the racing season here in Portland will be over."

Marge sat down again and slumped in her chair. "As far as I can tell, the season is never over around here. For the first time in my life, I swear I'll leave home if I don't hear something besides horse racing."

Hal took her hand. "You don't mean that."

"No, probably not." She shook her head. "But then I never dreamed my daughter would be racing thoroughbreds around the track either. And scaring me to death. Like an idiot, I thought we'd be doing a few girl-things together." She shook her head again. "Crazy, huh?"

Trish bit her lip. Would she and her mother *ever* see eye to eye?

CHAPTER 2

Gatesby was unhappy.

Trish stared the cantankerous bay right in the eye. "Now you listen to me." Her tone brooked no argument.

Gatesby snorted. He tossed his head and reached for her shoulder with bared teeth.

Trish smacked him on the nose with one hand and caught his halter with the other before he had time to jerk his head back. "I mean it. I have no time for your mule-headed, mean mood. Now you behave!"

Gatesby blew in her face as if to apologize. He dropped his head so she could reach his favorite scratching place. Trish obliged.

"You dunderhead. I don't know why we put up with you." She gave him another pat, clipped both lead lines to his halter and began a quick grooming so she could saddle him for the morning work.

Brad, part-time stable hand and full-time friend, kept his six-foot frame out of range of Gatesby's teeth. "Need any help?"

"Yeah, a few minutes ago. Where've you been?" Trish's smile took the sting out of her words.

"Sor-ry." Brad touched his fingers to the bill of his Seattle Sonics cap. "What can I do to help you, ma'am?"

Trish tossed him the brush. "You could finish while I go get the saddle."

Brad handed the brush back to her. "I'll get the saddle."

"Can't understand why nobody trusts you," she spoke to the colt as she slipped the bit into his mouth and the headstall over his ears. "Hard to believe you're the same ornery goof that greeted me."

"Now you be careful with him," Brad cautioned as he boosted Trish into the saddle.

"Brad, even *you're* beginning to sound like my mother. Is worrying a contagious disease?"

Brad sidestepped a sneaky nip by Gatesby. The look Brad flashed Trish spoke volumes.

Trish walked the colt out to the track at Portland Meadows. Dawn whispered its presence through a crack in the eastern cloud cover. The morning breeze, fresh from the rain during the night, carried the aroma of horse and hay and—Trish sniffed again. *Mm-m-m-m. Bacon already frying over at the cafeteria. If only I could spend all my mornings here at the track instead of rushing off to school.* She shrugged. *Well, at least Saturday is better than never.*

Gatesby pricked his ears and tugged at the bit.

"Sorry, fella, but the boss said walk today and jog the last lap. You get to run this afternoon."

————

And run he did. Gatesby hated dirt kicked in his face, so when Trish gave him some rein he surged around the outside as though the other horses were out for a Sunday trot. He won by a length and a half with his ears pricked forward and head up.

He didn't try to nip anyone until his owner, John Anderson, failed to pay attention to him in the winner's circle. When he turned his back on the colt he paid with a bruise.

"I swear he's laughing," Trish said after she scolded the colt. "Look at his eyes."

"I think I'd be better off watching his teeth," Anderson said, rubbing his shoulder. "You'd think I'd have learned by now. That was a good ride, Trish. You've really brought him along. Thanks, Hal." The two men shook hands and David trotted Gatesby back to the testing barn.

"See you later," Trish said as she headed for the dressing room. She had three more mounts on the day's program.

When she met her father for the ride home, she'd brought in a second win and a place, but her final mount faded at the six-furlong mark on the mile race.

"He just wasn't in condition." Trish tossed her sports bag in the back as she spoke. "What's wrong with trainers that don't keep their horses up to their peak?"

"Well, that one just wasn't ready after an injury. You know it takes time."

"Do I ever know. But then he shouldn't have entered the horse."

"True. But sometimes owners put the pressure on, Trish. You know there are countless reasons why a horse is entered—or scratched. Besides, what are you grumbling about?"

Trish flashed her father a guilty grin. "I hate not being in the money."

Hal chuckled. "I know how you feel."

"What do you think about Firefly? David's been keeping the ice packs on both her front legs, so she shouldn't have shin problems. We've made sure she's in peak condition."

"You never know." Hal shook his head. "Just happens sometimes, especially with two-year-olds. They're still growing, and racing too. We'll bring her home and give her plenty of rest."

And then she won't be ready for Santa Anita, Trish finished in her mind.

"Santa Anita is more than four months away." Her father read her thoughts again. "You know how things change for horses; you just do the best you can and pray for the rest. God cares about our business, Tee. You know that."

Trish nodded. Her father had such faith. Maybe strong faith came when you got old.

The next morning in church they sang Trish's favorite song. All the way home the words repeated in her mind. *"And He will raise you up on eagle's wings. . . ."* *We'll have to name a colt that sometime.*

All afternoon Hal looked like he was guarding a secret.

"All right, Dad, what's going on?" Trish nailed him as they walked back up from the barns.

"Whatever do you mean?"

"Da-ad!"

"Can't a person just be happy?"

"Sure. But you look like the night before Christmas."

"Well, Christmas *is* coming."

"That's not it and you know it."

"I'll never tell." Hal distracted her by pointing to a V-formation of Mallard ducks flying overhead. Their quacking echoed and drifted on the evening breeze.

The two stopped to watch as the birds angled west to the swamp beyond the horse pastures. Needle-topped fir trees stitched the sunset in place and a maple cradled a bird's nest in its naked arms. Caesar, their sable collie, shoved his nose into Trish's hand and whined softly.

Trish absently stroked his head, watching as the sun slipped its bindings and slept beyond the horizon. She inhaled the moment, then leaned her head against her father's shoulder.

"It's times like this I wish I were an artist." Hal hugged her with both arms and rested his chin on the top of her head. "God sure makes a wondrous world, doesn't He?"

Trish nodded, afraid words might break the spell. The molten gold of the sun flowed into pinks and fuchsia, washing the gray clouds with flaming color.

"Dinner's ready," Marge called from the house.

Trish and Hal turned, and with matching steps, arms locked, stepped over a puddle and kicked the mud off their boots before mounting the three concrete steps to the back deck.

Hal couldn't hide the twinkle in his eye through dinner. David and Trish exchanged puzzled glances. *What is going on?*

Marge hummed a little tune as she cut the apple pie she'd baked for dessert. "Anyone for a la mode?" She paused at the refrigerator door.

Trish groaned at the thought of the scale at the track. But then, she *was* down a pound or two—she shrugged as she glanced at her father. He nodded vigorously. Trish cast her "yes" vote along with the others. It had been a while since they'd had apple pie and ice cream.

"Well, Trish, do you have your report for the week?" Hal asked, savoring the pie.

She nodded. Each time her father asked for a report it brought back memories of when she'd ridden without permission. While the family meetings weren't always easy, even she had to admit that some of the strain had disappeared with everyone talking things out.

It's good to feel trusted, isn't it? her little voice whispered. Trish could only agree.

"I'm caught up on all my homework," Trish began. "And I've started one of the two papers due before Christmas break. I need to do some more research for the one on constitutional amendments before I begin writing."

"And your grades?" Marge took another sip of coffee.

"Nothing less than a B since I dropped Chemistry."

"Good." Hal smiled at her. "How many rides do you have this week?"

Trish ticked them off on her fingers for a total of 13. "And if we could get Anderson's gelding Final Command to want to win as much as he likes running *with* the winners, it'll be a great week."

Hal nodded. "Let me think on that. Marge?"

"I mailed the entries for both Santa Anita and the Kentucky Derby."

Trish knew how hard it was for her mother to do that. Marge had been against the idea of racing on distant tracks from the beginning. But she went along with the family decision. She'd also taken over all of the book-work and accounting since Hal had become sick.

Marge spoke again. "All the bills are paid and we have some money in the savings account again."

"Thanks to the two of you." Hal beamed at David and Trish. "Because of all your hard work, we have something special for each of you. David, you will now be on a regular employee basis. We'll pay you each week, just like we pay Brad and the other employees."

"Are you sure we can afford that, Dad?" David's eyes sparkled with hope.

"Yes, son. I'm just sorry it's taken so long. Maybe your missing college this year won't be a total waste—at least not financially."

"Thanks, Dad, Mom."

"And Trish, all the money you earn riding will be yours to keep."

"Dad!"

"That's right. You've been a tremendous help. And if we need money again—we know where to find you."

Everyone chuckled.

"Thanks!" Trish leaped from her chair to hug both her parents.

"That's not all." Marge picked up two envelopes. "These are for you too. Call it a bonus or reimbursement—whatever." She handed one to each of them.

Trish opened hers first. "Five hundred dollars!" Her mouth dropped open in shock. She stared at David. His look matched hers as he gaped at the check in his envelope.

Hal smiled. "You both earned it. I just wish it could have been more."

Marge cleared her throat. "You'll never know how much we appreciate you both and all that you've done." She reached across the table to squeeze their hands. "Thank you."

"Just in time for Christmas shopping!" David stuffed his check back in the envelope. "And my car needs new front tires. I'll stop by and check on prices tomorrow."

"Maybe you could drop Rhonda and me off at the mall at the same time." Trish pushed her chair back. She paused for David's nod before heading to the phone.

"We're on," she announced on her return. She hugged first her father, then her mother. "Thanks a lot. I wasn't sure what I was going to do about Christmas presents this year."

What to buy for each one whirled in her mind through dishes and homework. After shutting off the light in her room, she stared at the reflection of the yard-light on her ceiling. "Heavenly Father," she prayed, "help me find the perfect present for my dad this year. Something with *meaning*. And help me find it tomorrow. I don't have many chances to shop. And thank you for making him better. Amen."

A sweater? Huh-uh. Shirt and tie? Na-aa. New jacket? He sure needs one. Maybe. Trish fell asleep before the list got any longer.

The next day she turned more ideas over in her mind during her spare moments. It *had* to be the perfect gift.

"You're not going to spend *all* that money, are you?" Rhonda pushed her new glasses up on her nose.

"I don't know," Trish stuffed her books in her locker. "Let's get some lunch, I'm starved." For a change they were ahead of the crowd pouring into the lunchroom. They picked up their loaded trays and crossed the room to their favorite table.

Brad folded his lanky frame onto the stool next to Trish. "You two broke the speed record getting in here today. What's up?"

"Christmas."

"Not for over two weeks, last time I looked at a calendar."

Rhonda rolled her eyes and shook her head. "Shopping—you know, as in buying presents? I suppose you've got yours all done!"

"Right. And wrapped."

"Already?" Trish's voice squeaked in surprise. She coughed and took a swallow of milk to ease her throat.

"Hey, don't go into shock over it." Brad thumped her on the back. "Some of us have learned to be organized." He ducked the balled-up napkins they threw at him. "Can I help it if some of us are more perfect than others?" He leaned way back to avoid the milk Trish threatened to pour on his head. "Now, ladies." He held up both hands as if to fend them off. "Don't mess with me, you may get hurt you know."

"Ri-ght!" Trish picked up her tray. "Come on, Rhonda, we wouldn't want to get hurt, would we?"

A few minutes later they were combing their hair at the mirror in the restroom. No matter how much Trish brushed hers, the ebony strands bounced up around her face. She clipped the longest strands back and shoved her brush back into her purse. "Hurry out after class. David is meeting us right out front."

Rhonda picked up her purse. "We haven't gone shopping like this since before school started. We never have time for anything anymore."

Hours later, when Trish still hadn't found just the right gift for her father, she groaned as she shuffled the packages she'd already bought. "Let's get something to eat. I've about had it."

"Burgers or pizza?"

"Neither. Let's get a sandwich at Nordstroms. That's in about the middle of the mall."

Exhausted, they tucked their packages under the table and sank down in the chairs. "How come I get more tired shopping for a couple of hours than riding all day?" Trish rubbed an aching foot. "And I still don't have anything for my dad."

"Are you going to buy that turquoise ski jacket for yourself?" Rhonda asked just before the waitress brought their order.

"Depends on how much money I have left. That's over a hundred dollars—on sale." She took a long drink of her Diet Coke.

"It looked good on you."

"I know, and my other one's falling apart. Maybe I better put a new jacket on my Christmas list." She took a bite of her BLT. "What do I get my dad?"

They tossed ideas back and forth as they munched on chips. Nothing seemed just right; nothing was even close to right. Trish glanced at her watch. "We've got half an hour. Let's go."

She found it at the top of the escalator. Artists and craftspeople had set up booths throughout the mall, creating a holiday feeling. Trish almost walked on by. Sculptures weren't on her list of possibles.

But the eagle appeared to fly free. Each feather in the carved wood seemed alive, with the wind riffling through it. Trish stroked the eagle's head and across an extended wing. The grain of the wood lent color and depth. The song whispered through her mind, *Raise you up on eagle's wings* . . .

She was afraid to look for the price.

Rhonda picked the carving up and checked the sticker on the bottom. "Oooh-h." She flinched.

"How bad?"

"Two hundred dollars."

Trish closed her eyes. This was the perfect gift. She thought about the jacket she'd tried on. She couldn't afford both.

With a deep breath she pulled out her wallet. "Do

you have a box for the eagle?" she asked the woman behind the counter.

Trish tucked her prize down in middle of the Meier and Frank shopping bag. How could she keep such a secret till Christmas? Her dad had always guessed what she'd gotten him before. But not this year. This was the perfect gift. It would be a fantastic surprise.

But all surprises aren't so wonderful, as Trish learned after breezing Spitfire around the track on Wednesday.

"His right knee is hot," David informed her at the dinner table. "Did he stumble or anything when you were running him?"

CHAPTER 3

Spitfire's leg didn't get better.

Two days later, Trish trotted down to the barn as soon as she'd changed clothes. Each of the horses nickered at the sound of her voice. Dan'l tossed his head, begging for attention. Trish gave him a piece of carrot and stood rubbing his ears for a minute.

"You old sweetie, you." She stroked his nose and smoothed his coarse gray forelock. "I haven't ridden you for so long, I can't remember the last time." Dan'l rubbed the side of his head on her shoulder.

Next door, Spitfire banged a hoof against the door.

"Stop it, you'll re-injure that leg!" she ordered the pure black colt as she offered him his piece of carrot. The heavy canvas ice pack was still velcroed in place around his right foreleg. The pack reached from his ankle to well above the hot knee. Water leaked down over his hoof and into the straw.

Trish inhaled the familiar aroma of horse and straw with overtones of liniment. Spitfire draped his head over her shoulder, his eyes drooping as she rubbed his cheek and behind his ears. Firefly nickered for her turn, and beyond her Gatesby snorted and thumped the wall.

Caesar parked himself at Trish's knee, hoping for some attention too.

"You gonna just stand there moonin' around or what?" Brad's teasing voice broke into Trish's thoughts. "Where's David?"

"I don't know. His car was gone and Mom and Dad are off somewhere too." She gave Caesar a shove to get him off her foot. "I'll take Gatesby and you work Final Command, then I'll do Firefly and you can give Dan'l a gallop. He's been getting lazy lately."

"Yes, ma'am." He grinned at her. "Anything else, ma'am? You want me to—"

"Knock it off, is what I want." Trish shook her head as she entered the tack room. "Can't you ever be serious?"

"Maybe, why?"

"Oh, I don't know." She glanced back at him at just the wrong moment. Gatesby slipped in a quick nip and jerked his head up, ears back, ready for his scolding. "Ouch! Now see what you did?" This time she'd grabbed the horse's halter before yelling again at Brad.

Both Brad and Gatesby wore the same "Who me?" look.

Trish rubbed her upper arm one more time before Brad gave her a leg up.

"You watch him now." Brad unsnapped the lead shank as Trish straightened the reins.

"Thanks a lot—now. If I'da been paying attention to him earlier, I wouldn't have this bruise."

"Yeah, you'd think you'd have learned by now." Brad sidestepped as Trish nudged the colt forward. "Hey, you trying to make him step on me, by any chance?"

"Make him? Whatever gave you that idea?" Trish's laugh floated back on the breeze. "Hurry up and we can gallop together."

Spitfire looked clearly dejected when all the other horses were out and he still stood in the stall. Trish gave him some extra affection as she measured out his grain. "Sorry, fella, but you gotta get better. Maybe tomorrow David'll take you out for a walk."

After dinner that evening they finished decorating the noble fir that David and Marge had bought. When they placed the angel on the treetop, it nearly touched the slanted pineboard ceiling. A fire crackled in the fireplace; fat, red winterberry-scented candles flickered on the broad mantel, and Christmas carols drifted from the stereo.

"Needs something more on the left side," Hal pointed from his recliner. Marge attached a shimmery red bell and a revolving star to the branches he suggested and stepped back to inspect her handiwork. All the ornaments they'd collected through the years twinkled in their own special places.

Trish hung the last of the crocheted and starched snowflakes, then sank down, her legs crossed, in the middle of the floor. She propped her elbows on her knees and her chin on her fists, the better to gaze at the tree. Each year the ritual was the same and she loved every minute of it. She glanced over at the manger scene displayed on a low table to the side of the front window. When the tree lights went on, the star of Bethlehem above the stable would light up too.

Marge settled onto the arm of Hal's recliner. "Okay, David, turn them on."

For an instant Trish held her breath, then let it out as the twelve-foot tree shimmered into glory. "Oh-h-h, isn't it beautiful?" She felt the old, familiar tightening in her throat. All the colors, the special ornaments, the lights both twinkling on the tree and reflected in the window, all of the pieces came together to make each tree they'd had the most beautiful ever. She swallowed around the lump as she looked at her father. And most important, the family was all together.

Hal cleared his throat. "That's got to be the most perfect tree we've ever had."

"That's Mom's line," David said.

"Then I'll say it too," Marge replied softly. "Truly, this is our most beautiful tree ever." She laid her cheek on the top of Hal's head.

That night in bed Trish thought about their gathering around the tree. *We were all a bit weepy,* she thought. *But that's okay. Tomorrow night I'll put my presents under the tree.* She chuckled to herself. *And I'm not going to put name tags on them so no one can guess which is theirs.* She thought of the beautiful eagle wrapped in silver paper and a royal blue ribbon. *Dad'll never guess this time!*

With Christmas break only a week away, Trish burned the midnight oil to finish her two papers.

"Trish, it's after two o'clock," Marge said one night.

"I know, but I'm nearly done."

Marge frowned as she shook her head. "You know if you weren't riding so much, you'd have time for your studies. How many times have we reminded you that school *has* to come first?"

Trish gritted her teeth. "In case you haven't noticed, Mom, I didn't ride after school this week. I spent my extra time at the library."

"Well, you just can't leave things to the last minute like this."

"Right." Trish leaned back in her chair. She clamped her lips on the rest of the things she'd like to say. "Good night, Mom. These go in tomorrow, on time."

"I'll just have to make it up over vacation," she told Rhonda one evening on the phone. "Just think, I'll be able to ride the entire week-day programs, not just a couple of races after school. That way I can get my bank account back up."

"And since Christmas is on Monday, we can go shopping on Tuesday because you don't have racing that day. Maybe that jacket'll still be there."

Trish stretched as she hung up the phone. This was going to be a fantastic vacation! And tomorrow morning she'd be able to ride Spitfire around the track, even if it was only at a walk. His leg hadn't been warm for two days now.

"Can you help me with some more baking tomorrow?" Marge asked as Trish poured herself a glass of milk.

"Yep. I'll get the morning workouts done early, and I don't have to be at the track until two." Trish wished she hadn't mentioned the track when she saw a frown wrinkle her mother's forehead. "I'll have plenty of time. You haven't made sugar cookies yet and I'll do the Rice Krispies bars too."

"And fudge." David took the milk carton out of her hands. "We need lots of fudge." He poured his glass full and chose a brownie off the plate Marge had left on the counter.

"You can help us decorate the cookie trees and stars and stuff. You missed out last year," Trish told him.

"Just make extra fudge. With lots of nuts in it."

Marge and Trish laughed together at the silly grin on

David's face. "Seems to me we sent several care packages of fudge to you at college last year." Marge indicated the milk carton on the counter and pointed to the refrigerator.

"Yeah. And I had to fight off half the dorm to get any." David ducked his head as he reached for the carton to put it away. "I thought maybe Trish wanted more."

"Ri-ght!" Trish rinsed her glass in the sink and set it in the dishwasher. "See you in the morning, brother dear."

She paused a moment in front of the tree. *That is the most gorgeous tree we've ever had.* She heard her father cough as she passed his closed bedroom door. He'd gone to bed right after dinner. *God, please make him completely well*, she thought as she fell asleep.

Trish helped with the baking Saturday morning. The house smelled so good she hated to leave. At the track she'd already had one win before she joined her father and John Anderson in the saddling paddock. The gelding Final Command pricked his ears and blew in her face before rubbing his forehead on her silks.

Trish snapped rubber bands over her cuffs to keep the wind from blowing up her sleeves. While the sky was clear, the temperature was dropping and the wind felt like it was blowing right off a field of snow.

"Trish," John Anderson tapped her knee. "I want you to do something today that I know you're going to disagree with."

Trish stopped gathering her reins and stared first at John, then at her father. Her dad nodded.

"What is it?"

"I want you to use the whip on him. We all know that this old boy just likes to run with the bunch, so when you get him up with the front runners like you did last time, I want you to go to the whip. Make him *want* to win."

"But, but you know he—I . . ." Trish swallowed the rest of her argument. At her father's nod, she patted the horse's neck and unclenched her jaw. "If you say I have to."

As soon as they trotted on to the track, the wind knifed through Trish's winter silks and the long johns she wore. Her nose was already dripping as they passed the grandstand on the parade to post, and only the horse's warm neck kept her hands from freezing.

"Well, old boy," she said as he walked placidly into the starting gate. "Don't blame me, but they said we gotta light a fire under you. I promise you this, you run like we both know you can and I won't have to use the whip."

By the time the last stubborn horse finally entered the gate for the third time, Trish couldn't keep from shivering. But as soon as the gates clanged open and the field surged forward, she forgot the cold.

The gelding ran easily, about midway in the pack as the horses spread out by the halfway point. At Trish's urging, he gained on the fourth place, then the third.

"Come on now," she shouted at the four-furlong marker. "Go for it!" The gelding lengthened his stride to catch the second-place horse, hanging on the tail of the leader.

Trish hesitated for only an instant. She brought the whip down on his shoulder at the same time that she shouted, "Go!"

The gelding bolted forward. Trish whapped him again. With his ears flat against his head, the horse pounded across the finish line, nose and nose with the gray who'd been leading.

"A photo finish!" Trish galloped him a bit farther around the track before pulling him down and around. "Well, I guess we gave it our best shot. Maybe I should have given you the whip sooner."

The gelding shook his head. Trish kept an eye on the board as she walked him in circles. The icy wind sneaked past her concentration and made her shiver. *Man, it's cold.*

"And the winner is number five—" Trish ignored the rest of the announcement and trotted the gelding over to the winner's circle. She gave him one more pat as she slipped off.

"I hate to say I told you so, but—"

"He told you so," Hal finished, laughing. "Good job, Tee. We always knew this old bugger had a win in him."

"Congratulations and thanks," Anderson shook Trish's hand. "Just think, we don't even have to worry about bruises with this guy."

Trish hugged her saddle to block the wind when she stepped on the scale. And she still had another ride to go.

After a place in the eighth race, Trish jogged back to the stables to ride home with David and Brad. They had the gelding all loaded, but dusk was falling by the time they drove away from the track. David turned the heater on full blast when he felt Trish shiver beside him.

"Sure glad I'm not riding tomorrow if it stays this cold." Trish rubbed her hands in the warmth pouring from the vents. "Maybe we'll have snow for Christmas."

"That's all we need."

———

Trish got her wish. Thick snowflakes drifted down while the Evanstons enjoyed Christmas Eve dinner. By the time they left for church, the ground was white.

"At least it's warmer," Trish said as she slid into the backseat of the car. "And there's no wind."

"True." Hal pointed at the huge flakes sparkling past the yardlight. "Had to warm up to snow."

It was a candlelight service. Votive candles flickered in the iron sconces spaced along the walls. Tall white tapers banked the platform. Only the Christ candle remained to be lit on the cedar-bough Advent wreath suspended by chains behind the altar. White and gold chrismons and miniature white tree lights adorned the tall fir beside the pulpit.

Trish held her unlit candle while she glanced through the bulletin. All her favorite carols were being included in the service. She slipped her free hand through her father's arm. This was her most favorite service of the year.

A hush fell, as if all the world were waiting on tiptoe for the Christ Child to come. The organ burst into "Angels We Have Heard on High" and the congregation rose and began to sing as with one voice. Trish sang each "gloria," sure that the angels couldn't sound any better. The church was full to overflowing and so was her heart.

Outside after the service, Rhonda handed Trish a package wrapped in *Snoopy* paper. "Call me after you open your presents." She leaned close and whispered in Trish's ear. "Has he guessed yet?"

Trish shook her head. "Not even close." She gave Rhonda a narrow, flat box wrapped in silver paper. "Merry Christmas." After hugging Rhonda, she turned to give Brad his present when a snowball splooshed on her shoulder. She ducked the next one, this time from David, handed the package to Brad's mother, and scooped up the snow from the stair railing. Just as Brad turned, her barely packed snowball caught him on the cheek.

The fight flew fast and furious, quickly involving all the teenagers. Even an adult or two joined in and those that didn't cheered for the others.

David and Trish were still puffing when they joined their parents in the car after shouting "Merry Christmas" to everyone.

"Well, having a snowball fight is sure a different way to end the Christmas Eve service." Trish laughed as she slumped against the backseat and flicked a remaining clump of snow off on David.

By morning the snow had stopped falling, but all the fir trees drooped low with its weight. Trish and David hurried through the chores, making sure each horse got a handful of chopped carrots as a treat. Miss Tee preferred a handful of feed.

"Do you think we'll get more snow?" Trish asked as they slogged their way back up to the house.

"Possibly. Those clouds look mighty heavy." David kicked his boots against the steps. "Won't be much moving around today."

"Good. Let's hurry so we can open presents."

Marge had scrambled eggs with bacon and cheese ready when they walked through the door. Steaming mugs of hot chocolate with marshmallows were set at each of their places. The sliced round loaf of *Julekage*, Norwegian Christmas bread, was placed in the center of the table, flanked on either side with bright red candles.

"Oh, Mom," Trish breathed deeply. "This smells wonderful."

"Wash your hands and we're all set." Marge checked the table once more.

Hal bowed his head as they all joined hands. "Heavenly Father, all I can say is thank you. You have given us everything, but most importantly, you've given us yourself. Thank you for the food and for each other. Amen."

Trish squeezed both her mother's and David's hands. "Remember the year we got up at 3:30?"

"And I sent you back to bed with threats of no presents." Hal shook his head. "I'm sure glad you've learned to sleep in."

The meal couldn't pass quickly enough for Trish. But she knew the more she tried to hurry them, the slower her parents would be. "I get to be Santa this year." She gulped the last of her cocoa.

CHAPTER 4

You are the slowest people on earth, Trish thought.

"Patience, Tee." Hal smiled as he settled back in the comforting arms of his recliner.

"Is there any time you *can't* read my mind?"

"I'll never tell. Why don't you use some of that tamped down energy and throw another log on the fire?"

Trish put two logs on the fire while darting disgusted looks toward the kitchen where Marge and David dawdled with the dishes—or something.

"Maybe you should bring in a couple more chunks of wood before—"

"Da-ad."

Hal laughed. "Just kidding." He held up a hand in a plea for peace. "Come on in here, you two, before Trish has a conniption fit. You'd think something was under the tree for her the way she's carrying on."

That's not the problem this year, Trish thought. *This time I can't wait until you open your present from me.* She sank to the floor in front of the tree and hugged her knees. Sparks snapped their way up the chimney from the blazing fire. Strains from "O Holy Night" drifted from the stereo and mingled with the song about eagle's wings in Trish's mind.

She watched the gold disks of an ornament catch and

40

reflect the light as it revolved in the heat above a glowing red light bulb. The winged angel at the top seemed to smile right at her. Trish smiled back. This was a good morning for smiling.

"Here we are." Marge set a tray with steaming cups of hot chocolate on the coffee table. Roly-poly snowmen danced around each mug topped with whipped cream and a candy cane for stirring.

Trish crawled on hands and knees to the table, then sank back on her haunches. She shook her head. "You outdid yourself, Mom. How pretty."

"I thought we all needed something extra special today." She carried a mug over to Hal. "Here, dear. Merry Christmas." She leaned over and kissed him.

Trish watched them over the rim of her mug. The warm glow in the middle of her stomach had nothing to do with the hot chocolate. She hadn't even sipped it yet.

"Well, let's begin." Marge settled herself in her rocking chair and blinked away the tears that threatened to overflow and run down her cheeks. "Trish, let's start with the oldest first this year."

Trish searched the name tags for one for her father, then passed a shoebox covered with red and green holly paper to him. The tradition of each person opening a present while the others watched had begun. She planned to save the eagle for last.

David let out a yelp when he opened his first present. "Tires!" He waved the coupon in the air. "I haven't had time to buy mine yet."

"Good thing." Trish laughed along with him.

"Thanks, Mom, Dad."

Her laughter stopped when she opened a large flat box from her mother and father. "How did you know?

Rhonda told you—oh, it's beautiful." She held up the turquoise ski jacket with hot pink and white slashes on the sleeves. "Thank you, thank you," she repeated, hugging the jacket to her chest.

"Sorry you aren't happier with your present," Hal teased as he licked his candy cane. "This stuff sure is good, Marge."

The unopened gifts under the tree dwindled as the wrapping and ribbons littered the floor. Each one had opened several presents until only those for the neighbors were left—plus one. Trish drew the square silver box from behind the tree and carried it to her father.

"No tag?" He turned the box looking for a card.

"It's from me." Trish sank down on the hearth and leaned her elbows on her knees.

Hal carefully slit the paper.

"You *could* hurry a bit."

Please like it, the little voice inside her whispered.

Her father folded the paper and slit the tape on the heavy cardboard box.

Trish clenched her eyes and hands shut. The rustle of paper forced her to open them again.

Hal carefully lifted the eagle from its packing nest. He turned the burnished wood sculpture each way to look at it from every angle.

"Oh-h-h, Trish," Marge rose from her chair and knelt beside the recliner. "It's magnificent!"

Hal pressed his lips together and blinked rapidly. In spite of his efforts, a tear meandered down his cheek. He drew a forefinger across the lifted wing.

"D-do you—um-mm," Trish studied her father's face as he studied the eagle.

He likes it, you dummy, her little voice chanted. *Can't you tell?*

But Trish needed to hear his approval. "Well?" her voice steadied this time.

Hal handed the eagle to Marge and reached both arms for his daughter. "Thank you, Tee," he said into her hair as he gathered her close to his chest. "Where did you ever find anything so perfect?"

"You—you said that was your favorite verse, too." Her voice was muffled against his shirt. "And the song, it keeps playing in my head."

David took the eagle from Marge so he could examine it. "It's really something. Each feather is carved so perfectly. It looks alive."

"Remember when we saw the eagle flying up the gorge?" Marge said, taking the bird from David and handing it back to Hal. "Looking at this, I can almost hear it screeching. Thanks, Trish, for something we can all enjoy."

Trish rested her elbows on the arm of the chair and watched her father study the bird again. A smile flitted from his eyes to mouth and back again. "So wild and free," he murmured as he finally set his gift on the table by his chair. Light from the brass reading lamp made the burnished wood glow even more.

"Merry Christmas, everyone." Hal's smile lingered a bit longer on Trish. "And thank you all." He stroked the soft wool of the heather green sweater David had given him. "And now, are there any refills on that delicious chocolate, Marge?" He hoisted his mug. "All this makes a man thirsty." Eyeing the platter of cookies he said, "And hungry."

"Why don't you pick up in here, Trish, while I get the refills going?" Marge caught Trish's glance at the fireplace. "And don't throw it all in there. We don't need another chimney fire."

"That one was David's fault." Trish pulled herself to her feet and followed her mother into the kitchen. "Do you think he *really* liked it?" she whispered as she pulled two folded grocery bags from the rack under the sink.

"Oh, Trish, how can you doubt it?" Marge shook her head as she reached to hug her daughter. "He—I almost cried too. The eagle was absolutely perfect." Marge leaned back so she could look Trish in the eye. "Did it take *all* your money?" she whispered.

Trish shook her head. "Not *all* of it. It's just a good thing I'll have more coming from the track next week. But once I saw it, I just *had* to buy it. I'd been praying for that special gift and there it was." A grin turned up the corners of her mouth. "And besides, it was 25% off."

"So you got a bargain, then." Marge smiled as she filled the teakettle at the sink.

"Well, you taught me to be a careful shopper." Trish ducked away from the playful swat aimed at her.

After they'd straightened the living room, and the presents were neatly arranged under the tree, Hal finished his hot chocolate and stretched his arms over his head. "How about the two of you letting the horses out in the pasture to play in the snow. They'll enjoy it as much as you did the snowball fight last night."

"Miss Tee, too?"

"Of course. Give her a taste of winter. And David, keep an eye on that mare. She isn't due until about the tenth but she's a sneaky one. She'll head for the far corners when she's ready to foal. I think I'd better keep this chest out of that cold. I'll help your mother with dinner."

Marge rolled her eyes. "Thanks a whole lot."

David and Trish looked at each other and laughed. Everyone knew that Hal was *not* a cook. "See if you can keep from burning the potatoes this time," Trish called as she headed down the hall to change.

Caesar barked a welcome when they opened the sliding glass door. Puffy snow blanketed the deck and pillowed on the hanging baskets. A blue spot peeked from between the low-flying clouds, but to the west, heavy gray clouds promised more snow.

"We'd better hustle." David nodded at the sky. "I'll feed the outside stock while you let the racing string out." With the collie bounding through the snow beside them, the two followed their early morning tracks to the stables.

"I'll let Miss Tee out first and then the others." Trish gave Caesar a push, then tried to leap ahead of him. When he bounded back at her, she tried to sidestep but slipped and fell on her back in the snow. The collie put both feet on her chest and swiped a couple of licks across her nose.

She grabbed his white ruff and rolled him off her. With her laughing and Caesar's barking, the entire stable erupted with whinnies and hoof slammings.

David quit trying to be heard. He put two fingers in his mouth and blew hard. A piercing whistle split the icy air.

Trish started to giggle. Caesar quickly licked her chin. The giggle turned to a hoot. When she finally quit laughing, she could hardly get her breath. She raised up on her elbows, shaking the snow off her stocking cap. Caesar sat beside her, his tail feathering the snow, and like a perfect gentleman, he extended one paw.

Trish crashed again, overcome by giggles.

Spitfire whinnied, a high, demanding cry for some of the attention she was wasting on the dog.

David stood over her, arms crossed, trying to either keep or regain a straight face. "Do you think you could come help me before dark, at least?"

Trish scooped a handful of snow and tossed it at him. When another caught Caesar full in the face, she crossed both arms above her head to protect herself, both from her brother and the dog.

David reached down and hauled her to her feet. "Come on, snow bunny, we've got work to do."

"Want to make angels?" Trish punched him in the side. "Or are you too grown up for snow angels?"

Old gray Dan'l stretched his neck out as far as the closed stall door would allow. He nickered, a plea for attention impossible to ignore.

"Nope, but explain the wait to your friends there."

Trish dug pieces of carrot out of her pocket and gave each horse both a treat and a pat as she went down the line. "Be right back," she promised before she headed across to the old barn.

Miss Tee plowed to a stop when her hooves hit the snow. She bent to sniff, then tossed her head when the cold touched her muzzle.

"Come on, silly," Trish called as she led the mare out to the paddock. Miss Tee raised each foot high, trying to step over the cold powder. She leaped but still found herself up to her knees when she came down. Then the filly discovered the best way was to follow her mother's trail.

Trish gave her baby an extra pat as the filly finally tiptoed through the gate. The mare immediately buckled her knees and rolled back and forth, grunting in pleasure.

Miss Tee stood stock still. If horses could talk, her

look said it all; she was sure her mother had lost her mind.

Trish laughed her way back to the row of stalls where the racing string waited. One by one, she led them out to the board-fenced pasture. And just like the mare, each of them rolled and scratched, then shook all over upon standing up.

They snorted and blew, tossed their heads and charged across the snowy field, just like a group of kids let loose from school on a snow day. Trish leaned on the fence, enjoying their antics. *If only you could see them, Dad*, she thought. *You need a good laugh too.*

You can be thankful he's alive, her nagging little voice said as if perched on the snow-capped fence post beside her. *You know he . . .*

"Oh shut up." Trish spun on her heel and headed up to the barns. "Mucking out stalls is better than listening to you." Caesar cocked an ear. "No, I'm not talking to you." She tugged his ruff. "And I'm not going crazy either."

Snowflakes began drifting down again by the time they had all the stalls clean and the animals back in and fed. The twinkling lights of the Christmas tree in the front window beckoned them back to the warmth. The aroma of baked ham met them at the door, along with their mother's voice.

"Dinner in about fifteen minutes. I've made spiced cider to warm you up."

Trish hung her jacket in the closet and laid her gloves and hat on the warm air vent to dry. She glanced in the living room. Her father's chair was empty. "Where's Dad?"

"Sleeping. He'll be up in a few minutes."

"Sure smells good in here." David pulled off his boots at the jack by the door. "Here, Tee, hang up my jacket too."

"Did you ever hear the word please?" She stood with her hands on her hips.

David dumped the denim coat over her head. "Please. And thank you. In advance."

Trish pulled the thing off her head, muttering around the grin she tried to keep hidden. "Muck the stalls, hang up my coat; you don't want a sister, you want a slave."

"Oh, and could you pour me a mug of that cider?"

David sidestepped her punch and laughed his way down the hall to his room.

That night, after spending nearly an hour on the phone with Rhonda, Trish snuggled down in her bed. *No homework, a day that can never be topped, extra rides coming up to pad my bank account, and best of all, no school for nine days!* And tomorrow she and Rhonda were going shopping and to a movie. That is, if the roads cleared.

If only Dad didn't have to go to the hospital tomorrow for another treatment.

CHAPTER 5

"Mom says I can't drive." Rhonda moaned over the phone the next morning.

"I know. The roads are just too slick. David's taking Mom and Dad to the hospital in the four-wheel drive."

"Another treatment?"

"Yeah. About the time he's feeling pretty good, they knock him down again. Just going outside in the cold air made him start coughing." Trish slid to the floor so she could lean back against the cupboard. "Why don't you walk over and help me and Brad with the chores."

"Thanks a lot. I wanted to go shopping."

"Mm-mm. You coming or not?"

"All right."

Trish didn't mind staying home. She didn't have much money left, and now she didn't need to buy a jacket. "And you don't really *need* anything else," she reminded the face in the mirror as she brushed her hair. A movie and lunch out would have been nice. And who knew when they'd have time for that later.

She finished straightening up her room, tossed the dirty clothes in the washing machine and shrugged into her jacket. A quick check outside and she switched from leather boots to rubber ones. It had begun to rain.

"You be careful out there," Brad cautioned as he

boosted her into the saddle on Spitfire.

"No problem, we're just walking today. Rhonda's coming over so why don't you saddle Firefly for her. If you'd like, you could work Anderson's Final Command."

"That's okay. I'll get the stalls cleaned out. Then we'll all be done about the same time. Maybe we'll get to that movie yet, the way the snow's melting."

Spitfire shied when a load of snow swooshed off a fir branch and thwunked in the snow. He spooked again when another tree dumped its load. Trish hunched her shoulders to keep the drizzle from trickling down her neck but never took her attention from the frisky horse. She stroked his neck with one hand and kept up a running commentary on all she saw. He settled after one round of the track and seemed as relieved as she when they turned back to the stables.

"Better late than never," Trish teased her friend who'd arrived while Trish stripped the saddle off Spitfire in his stall. "You want Gatesby or Firefly?"

Rhonda gave her a have-you-lost-your-marbles look.

Brad chuckled as he boosted the slender redhead into the saddle. "So you don't want a blue-and-green from Gatesby, eh?"

Rhonda stared down at him from Firefly's back. "A blue-and-green?" She started to laugh. "That's a good one, Brad. No, I don't want a Gatesby bruise, or to get dumped either. I don't know how Trish puts up with him."

"With who?" Trish stopped Final Command in front of Firefly's stall.

Gatesby nickered in the stall next to them. To look at the blaze down his long face and the soft eyes, no one would guess him to be ornery, until he laid back his ears and reached for Trish's jacket.

"Him!" Brad backed up the gelding so his back was out of range of Gatesby's nipping teeth. He gave Trish a leg up. "You should have put him on the hot walker to work off some of his meanness."

"I'm starved." Brad closed the door and shot the bolt on the tack room when they were finished. "I'll go home and change, then we can go."

"I gotta call my mom first. She'll probably say okay now that it's warmed up and I'm not driving." Rhonda sniffed. The cold had made her nose run too.

"Well, we better hurry. I have to be home in time to feed, in case David doesn't get back. We could get hamburgers at the drive-in window at Burgerville. That way we can make the matinee." Trish pushed open the sliding glass door. While they waited for Rhonda to call home, she slipped out of her jacket and hung it over the back of a chair to dry. "Want a cookie, Brad?"

"Just one?"

"No, you nut. The whole plate. I don't care how many you eat. Help yourself. Mom musta known you were coming. She left some of each kind."

"Man, oh man!" Brad popped a brownie in his mouth while he picked out several other kinds. "Your mom is the best baker."

"Hey, she didn't do it all. I helped."

Brad pretended to gag.

"Don't worry. She made the brownies. Just don't try the Rice Krispies bars. I did those."

"I can go!" Rhonda gave a little skip as she entered the room. She looked down at her wet jeans. "You got some clothes I can borrow?"

"See you in fifteen minutes." Brad swallowed the last

of his cookies and grabbed a couple more. "To keep me from passing out." He laughed as he went out the door.

––––––––––

They slid into their seats just as the opening scenes of the matinee appeared on the theater screen. Brad passed the popcorn tub over to Trish and pulled off his jacket. After propping his knees on the seat-back in front of him, he pushed up his sleeves and reached for some popcorn.

"You think you can settle down now?" Trish whispered.

"Sure, who's got the Coke?" He popped a handful of popcorn in his mouth. "Anybody get napkins?"

"Shush," Rhonda giggled as she handed him the tall drink. "We should never let you out in public."

"Hey, I'm driving, remember?"

A woman in front of them turned to frown at Brad.

Trish was afraid to look at Rhonda for fear they'd never be able to quit laughing. It was a good thing the movie was a comedy. It was a giggly kind of afternoon.

But that night Trish didn't feel like laughing. Her father had been throwing up for five hours straight. In between that he had coughing spells.

By the time Hal finally fell into an exhausted sleep, Trish felt like her own throat was raw. "I thought they'd found some medicine that would keep him from being so sick." She slumped in her dad's recliner with her feet across the arm so she could warm her toes by the fire.

"This time none of that seems to help." Marge leaned her head back in the rocking chair. "I think the cold air made things worse because it started the coughing."

"Just when he was finally feeling better, too."

"I know. But at least he is getting better. We've got to be thankful for that."

"Mm-mmm." Trish bobbed her toe to the beat of "The Little Drummer Boy" on the stereo. "It just doesn't seem fair."

"I think that storm is hitting earlier than they predicted," David said, entering the room to rub his hands in front of the fire. "I've just been down to check on the animals. I think it's dropped about twenty degrees out."

"Is it still raining?" Marge asked.

"More like sleet now. I turned the light on in the pump house and blanketed all the racing stock."

"We'd better store up some water in case the electricity goes out. Trish, you could fill the bathtub. I'll fill some jugs in the kitchen. Want some hot chocolate, David, or coffee?"

———

When Trish tiptoed in to kiss her father good night, she had to hold back a sob. His gray look was back, in fact his face looked almost green. Dark shadows shrouded his eyes and hollowed his cheeks. The curved plastic basin on the nightstand was a grim reminder of hospital days.

"I love you," she whispered as she dropped a kiss on his forehead. Her father's eyelids flickered and he nodded ever so slightly, as if any movement might bring on the vomiting again.

Trish met her mother in the doorway of the bedroom.

"Don't worry, Tee. He'll be better tomorrow."

Trish wished her mother's words carried more conviction. And who was *she* to say not to worry?

Trish chewed her bottom lip as she entered her own

bedroom. Her gaze went to the verses printed on the cards she'd pinned on the wall: ". . . on eagle's wings."

She spun out the door and back to the living room. The carved eagle stood on the mantelpiece, its wings spread wide over the pine boughs. Trish carefully lifted it down and went to the door of her parent's bedroom. Marge was holding a straw to Hal's mouth so he could sip a drink. The room was dim with only the light of a small lamp on the nightstand.

Trish tiptoed around the end of the bed and made room for the eagle near the lamp. A smile lifted the corners of her father's mouth as he whispered, "Thanks."

Trish awoke sometime during the night to put another blanket on her bed. She closed the small crack in the window that she always left open. No more snow fell in the circle of the yardlight. At least that was good news. She snuggled back into her bed and fell into a deep sleep.

———

The next day was dark and foreboding. Clouds hovered, shading from gun-metal gray to pussy willow. A biting wind whistled through the bare trees as David and Trish took care of the animals. All racing had been canceled due to the weather.

"Dad looks terrible," Trish blurted, slamming the bucket down in the tack room.

"At least he's not coughing or throwing up," David tried to console her.

"Yeah, thank God for small favors."

"Knock it off, Trish. Mom said—"

Trish spun around and glared at her brother. "I don't care *what* Mom said. She should have left him at the hospital where someone could help him."

"She tried. Dad wouldn't stay."

"Oh." Trish felt like crawling under a tack box.

"If you're through with your temper tantrum, maybe we should go up for dinner, before Mom comes down to see what happened to us."

"Sorry." Trish closed the door behind them. A few minutes ago she would have slammed it. And that would have startled the horses. They didn't like having both halves of their doors closed anymore than she did. And right now Trish felt like all kinds of doors were closing on her.

The wind slashed at their jackets and snapped at their faces all the way to the house. Trish caught herself when she slipped on the sidewalk. Sliding could be fun, but not now.

"If that wind would just die down, I'd sprinkle some ashes on the sidewalk and steps," David said. "You almost went down."

"I'm just glad I don't have to go out again tonight." Trish gave Caesar a pat. "Do you think we should bring him in?"

"No. He's got a good, warm doghouse. You'll be fine, won't you boy?" David rubbed the dog's ears and scratched the white ruff. Both he and Trish stamped the snow off their boots before they stepped inside.

"Dad's still in bed," Marge said before Trish had a chance to ask. "But he did eat some chicken noodle soup."

Trish felt the sadness lift, just a bit.

"Now how about ham sandwiches and chicken noodle soup for you two? It's all ready. You look frozen. Get in front of the fire and I'll bring it to you on trays."

Trish shivered when she took her jacket off, then sat

down on the hearth with her back as close to the crack-
ling logs as she dared.

Marge handed her a steaming mug of soup. "Maybe
this will help."

Trish felt much better when she was finally warm,
had eaten, and checked on her father. Some color had
returned to his cheeks and he was breathing more easily.

Pulling her quilt up over her shoulders in her own
bed, Trish waited for her body heat to warm the sheets,
then said her prayers. It was easier to thank God when
her dad looked better.

When daylight came, she stuck her nose out of the
covers. The room was cold even with the window closed.
She glanced at her clock. It had stopped at two. No electricity! Trish threw back the quilt and sprinted to the
window. The tree branches hung low to the ground,
buckling under a blanket of ice. Even the cars were en-
tombed.

Trish's world was frozen over.

CHAPTER 6

"Come on, Tee. I need help." David tapped on her door.

"What's wrong?" David was down the hall before Trish could ask any more. "Besides no electricity, that is," she muttered as she pulled on her long johns, then jeans. "Man, it's cold in here!"

"Where's David?" Trish pulled a sweater over her head as she entered the living room.

"He said to find him in the pump house. He's trying to get the generator going." Marge closed the glass doors on the roaring fire, then stood and rubbed her hands together. "At least we can heat part of the house."

"How's Dad?"

"He's okay. I wanted to get it warm out here before he gets up."

Trish pulled on her jacket, a stocking cap and gloves. She grabbed a flashlight and stepped out the sliding door. The wind caught her as she rounded the corner. She pulled her collar up as far as it would go and headed for the pump house that squatted on the rise halfway to the barns.

"I've never seen so much ice," she said as she bent down at the open door. David was kneeling inside, tinkering with the red gasoline generator. "Here's another flashlight. What can I do to help?"

"This blasted thing won't start. Dad's the one with the magic touch. If I don't get it going pretty soon, the pump will freeze and we'll really be in trouble." David slammed a wrench onto the concrete. "I'm just not a good mechanic." He tucked his bare hands under his armpits.

"Didn't you bring gloves?"

"Sure, but I can't work with them on." His breath blew out in puffs, even inside the tiny building.

Trish knew to keep her mouth shut. David's anger wasn't directed at her. It took a lot to get him angry, but when he did—

"Hold that light so I can see over here."

Trish hunkered down and tried to direct the beam to where David indicated.

"Trish, for Pete's sake, can't you hold that thing still?"

Trish swallowed a retort.

"Hand me that screwdriver."

Trish looked through the array of tools in the toolbox and spread out on the floor. "Which one?"

"The Phillips."

She passed him the first one she saw.

"Not that one, the big one with the brown handle."

She passed it to him, but in doing so lowered the beam of light.

"Thanks a lot. Now I can't see anything. Can't you at least keep the light in the right place?"

Trish clamped her teeth together. *You try to do both and see how you do, brother,* she thought.

"Okay, see the pull cord?"

"Yes."

"It pulls hard so give it all you've got."

Trish set down the light, grasped the wooden grips and jerked hard. She banged her head on the top of the door frame and sat down thump in the snow, the cord in her hand. "Ow-w-w!" She blinked back the tears that surged in response to the blow on the back of her head.

"What happened? You okay, Trish?" David crawled from behind the generator and stuck his head out the door.

Trish held up the cord with one hand and rubbed the spot on her head with the other. She was glad her mother wasn't there to see their predicament.

"What are we gonna do?"

"I don't know." David crawled the rest of the way out and rose to his feet. He kicked the door closed and turned the knob. "Maybe Dad can come look at this thing. We better get that tank loaded on the truck and go get some water. All the animals need a drink and I know the water troughs must be frozen.

"You go get the pick-up and I'll start the tractor."

Trish blinked against the pain in her head and handed David the broken cord. "Here, we better not lose this." She extended a hand for him to pull her to her feet. "Wow, that was a shocker."

"You okay?"

"Yeah, great. I feel like my head is separated from my body, I'm freezing cold, and I love having you holler at me. Anything else? Sure, I feel great."

"Sorry, Tee. The keys are in the truck."

Trish rubbed her head again before stuffing her gloved hands into her pockets. *What a miserable morning. And what a vacation!*

When she tried to open the truck door, it wouldn't

budge. She couldn't push the button in. She tried again. Nothing. She slammed her hand against the door. Still nothing. *Is it locked? No, the button is up.*

She went around to try the other door. Both of them were frozen shut.

Then she heard the roar of the tractor coming to life. *Well, at least something's working around here.* She carefully made her way down to the barn, watching the icy patches. She didn't need another bruise.

"The truck doors are frozen," she announced.

David slammed his hand against the steering wheel. "What more can go wrong?" He shut off the tractor and leaped to the ground. "Let's hope Mom has some water heating in the fireplace."

Whinnies and nickers from behind the closed stall doors meant a plea for both light and morning feed.

"Why don't I take care of these guys while you go thaw out the truck door?" Trish nodded toward the stables. At David's okay, Trish went down the line, opening doors on her way to the feed room. Horse heads popped out like jack-in-the-boxes, all of them eyeing Trish like they hadn't been fed in days.

Trish filled the two five-gallon feed buckets and set them in the wheelbarrow along with the remainder of a bale of hay. Each time she swung the lower half of a stall door open she had to push by an eager horse to get to the manger.

"Where are your manners this morning?" she complained as Spitfire snatched a mouthful of grain from the scoop. "What's gotten into all of you?"

She grabbed Gatesby's halter with one hand, then poured his grain and tossed hay in the rack with the other. "Sorry, guy, I don't feel like any new bruises today. I already got my share." In each stall she checked the water buckets. Those that weren't dry were chunks of ice.

By the time she finished with the outside stock and Miss Tee, she could feel her own stomach rumbling. Caesar didn't seem to mind the cold wind as he danced beside her. "Sorry, no time to play," she said when he crouched in front of her with nose on his front paws and plumy tail waving in the air.

"What's the hold up, David?" she called when she walked back into the house. Closed off from the living room, the kitchen was cold, but it sure beat the wind outside. Trish stamped the snow off her boots and stepped into the living room where the fire blazed in the hearth. She pulled off her gloves and extended her hands to the warmth. The cast-iron teakettle rested on its metal frame to the side of the burning logs.

"Morning, Tee," Hal said from the comfort of his recliner. "You look about frozen."

"Hungry too, I'm sure," Marge added.

"Yeah, I am. Where's David?" She tossed her jacket at the sofa.

"He's waiting for the water to heat so he can thaw out the truck doors." David stepped into the room as Marge spooned instant cocoa powder into a mug.

"And I'm going to see if I can't get that blasted generator running." Hal spoke over his mug of coffee.

"Dad, you shouldn't go out . . ." Trish's comment faded away at the glare from her brother. *Looks like they've already had a discussion about that.* Her thoughts finished her sentence. *You shouldn't go out in that wind and cold.* She wanted to tie her dad to the chair.

"Why don't you wait until I get back with the water tank so I can help you." David shrugged into his jacket.

"Trish can water the animals while we fix the generator."

"Heard anything from Brad?" Trish turned so her backside would warm up at the fire.

"Can't. The phone's down, too. They've probably got about the same situation we do. Thought I'd swing by there on the way in to town in case I can fill the tank there." David brought a half-bucket of water from the bathtub and added water to it from the steaming teakettle. "Got a pitcher, Mom?"

Marge spoke as she searched the cupboard for a larger pitcher. "Trish, get some cereal, and there's juice in the fridge. Dad's been toasting bread on the long forks, if you want some. Here you go, David. Anything else?"

"Yeah, warmer weather." He pulled on a hat and gloves and left with the bucket and pitcher.

Trish got her breakfast and huddled on the raised hearth to keep warm while she ate. Her dad offered her some of the bread he'd toasted. "Mm-mm. Thanks, Dad. That's really good. Sure beats toast done in the toaster."

"At least I'm good for something around here."

Trish caught the insinuation that her father felt helpless, even though he smiled when he spoke. She glanced at her mother and father, catching a look that passed between them. While Marge kept her opinions to herself, Trish knew her mother was really worried. And this time she had real reason to be.

"How are things down at the barn?" Hal sounded raspy and short of breath.

"Fine. The horses are frisky, wired. They don't like having their stall doors closed."

"Too bad. How's your head?"

Trish felt for the bump. "Saw stars for a minute. Probably should have put some snow on it but I was already too cold. That wind is awful."

"The radio says more of the same, and colder tonight. They're sanding the main roads, but you could help David put chains on the truck. With those and the four-wheel drive, he ought to be able to get to Orchards and back if he drives slowly." Hal coughed carefully.

The truck roared to life out in the driveway. "Well, that's one problem solved." Trish drank the last of her hot chocolate. "You need anything from the store, Mom?" she asked as she bundled into her gear.

"No, thanks." Marge rubbed her elbows as she stared out the front window. She turned and forced a smile. "Now you be careful."

How often have I heard those words? Trish thought as she slipped her way down the sidewalk. Right now, her father was the one who needed to be careful. He didn't need all this cold and extra worry. And he certainly shouldn't be out working on the generator. *God, you've sure sent this crummy weather at a bad time. Do you have something against us?*

David had pushed the truck seat forward and was pulling the chains out when Trish reached him. He handed her a chain. "Here, just lay this out behind the back wheel and make sure everything is straight. Then we'll back over the chains and hook 'em on."

Trish did as she was told and miraculously it worked. David only got angry once when one of the links refused to close. At least he had plenty of light to work with. Trish was about to tease him but one look at his face told her to keep her comments to herself.

"Okay," he grunted as he pulled himself up by the rear bumper. "Now let's get that tank loaded."

Within a few minutes they had strapped the tank to

the bucket of the power lift on the front of the old red tractor and hoisted it above the pick-up bed.

"Now when I get it lowered in place, you release those straps," David instructed. "Make sure you keep your hands and feet out of the way because that tank'll roll."

You sound more like Mom every day. Worry, worry, worry, Trish grumbled to herself as she climbed up over the pick-up bed. She leaned over and tugged on the strap catches.

Nothing happened.

"Get over here by the bucket. That'll give you more leverage."

Trish squeezed by the head of the 500-gallon tank and braced herself against the tractor bucket. She reached over, snagged the black webbing and pulled.

The strap released.

Trish hung in the air for a fleeting moment. Her arms windmilled to try to catch her balance, but the ice on the fender sent her toppling to the ground.

"Ooooff."

"I told you to be careful!" David leaped down from the tractor. "Are you all right?"

Trish took a deep breath. And let it all out. This getting dumped on her butt was beginning to get to her. "I'm fine, David. Just fine."

He reached a hand down to pull her to her feet. "You sure you're not hurt?"

"No, at least the snow is good for cushioning." She brushed the snow and ice off her backside. "How's the water tank?"

David climbed up and released the other strap so the tank could roll into place. "Do you think you can back the tractor up without getting into trouble?"

Trish stuck her tongue out at him as she stepped aboard the tractor, released the gear on the hoist and backed the bucket away from the truck. She shifted gears, drove the tractor back to the barn and parked it in the center aisle just down from Miss Tee's stall.

She stopped a moment to rub the filly's forehead. A few white hairs swirled a miniature star between the baby's eyes. Trish kissed the soft muzzle. "No time to play today, but you be good." She patted the mare. "I'll bring you a drink pretty soon."

"Tri-ish!"

"I'm coming." She trotted out of the barn, being careful not to slip on the ice. She didn't need another spill.

The temperature seemed to be dropping by the time they got back with the load of water. David parked the truck at the stables and both of them filled buckets from the spigot on the bottom of the tank and poured water into all the horses' water buckets.

Then they drove out to the aluminum water troughs in the pastures. Since those all had automatic floats, the tanks were full—of solid ice. David leaned his head on his hands on the steering wheel. He took a deep breath.

"I'll go get the pickax," Trish scooted out the door before he could even ask her.

The ice was only about six inches thick, so chopping through it didn't take as long as she'd feared. The mares and yearling stood in a semi-circle watching the action until Trish brought them each a bucket of water while David chopped. The horses drank deeply.

But the Hereford beef stock in the next pasture were too spooked to drink from the buckets. Their plaintive moos begged David to chop faster. When the water was clear, they pushed and shoved to get their turn.

"We'll empty both of these when they're done and then water them again tonight. That way the troughs won't freeze up." David climbed back into the truck. "I'm going to take some of this up to the house and fill the bathtub again. So we'll have water for the house."

Trish slammed the door after joining him. "You know, Davey boy, you're pretty sharp."

He shot her a quizzical look.

"The way you seem to know all the right stuff to do."

"I couldn't get the generator going."

"No, but like dumping the troughs. I never would have thought of that."

"Just common sense." David parked the truck as close to the house as he could. He smiled at her. "Thanks, Tee."

David and Hal were still struggling with the generator when Trish went down to the barn to feed and water the animals again. Darkness was falling when she got back up to the house.

"Did you empty the hauling tank?" David asked.

"No, I didn't think of it." Trish turned and went back outside. She opened the valve and watched as the water drained out on the ground, freezing as it formed a puddle. She wrapped both arms around herself to keep out the biting east wind that whipped down the gorge, bringing the cold from the Rockies. When the trickle stopped, she closed the handle and trudged back to the house.

"No luck, huh?" She asked David after removing all her gear.

"No." David shook his head. "And when we called about renting a generator, they were all gone. Besides that, now we'll have to thaw out the pump, too. And who knows how many pipes are frozen."

"How's Dad?"

"Terrible."

CHAPTER 7

"I told him he shouldn't try to fix it."

"I know, David," Marge spoke softly so as not to wake Hal, who slept soundly in the recliner. "I tried to tell him too, but you know how stubborn your father is. He was determined to fix that generator."

"I'll take it in to be repaired tomorrow." David rubbed his hands over his forehead and through his hair.

"Just buy a new one. Your father kept that thing running with baling wire and chewing gum. It's time to lay it to rest."

"Why, Mom, I—"

"We'll deal with your father later. I should have had the nerve to say this earlier today and saved him all this." Marge waved her hand toward her husband.

She'd spread a comforter over the recliner, then a quilt and another comforter. With all that it still took a long time for him to get warm.

Trish listened to their conversation with one ear and kept the other tuned to her father's shallow breathing. Even with the help of the oxygen tank by his chair, she could hear the struggle. And with the oxygen he couldn't be close to the fireplace, so they'd moved the recliner over by the sofa.

He looks shrunken in those quilts, Trish thought. *I*

thought you were helping us, God! He keeps telling us you're making him well, but he sounds awful. She chewed her lip to hold back the tears.

Hal coughed then, a deep wrenching cough that shook the chair.

"Here, Dad." Trish unwrapped a throat lozenge and held it to his mouth. "This'll help."

Hal nodded. His eyes fluttered open and a tiny smile lifted one corner of his mouth. "Thanks, Tee." His eyes closed again. "Don't worry. I'll be better in the morning."

"I'll take the sofa and you two get your sleeping bags," Marge said after settling Hal into the chair for the night. "The bedrooms are much too cold and at least we can keep the fire going in here. Trish, get some quilts and you can use them as pads under the bags."

The glow from the kerosene lamp looked warm but didn't make a difference in the arctic bathroom. By the time Trish had brushed her teeth, she was glad to get back into the living room.

The candles on the mantel, the two lamps, and the glow from the fireplace held them all in a circle of light. Trish looked up at the angel on the tree. She couldn't see its smile tonight; in fact, she could hardly see the angel in the dimness. It didn't surprise her.

She snuggled down into her sleeping bag.

"Our Father, who art in heaven . . ." Marge said softly after blowing out the lamps. Hal's whisper could barely be heard as he joined in the prayer.

Trish felt like plugging her ears. She was glad when they said "Amen."

How would she ever be able to go to sleep, listening to her father fight to breathe?

"Trish. Trish!" David shook her.

"Wha—what's the matter?" Trish pulled the sleeping bag off her head.

"I'm taking Mom and Dad in to the hospital. He's started to run a temperature."

Trish shoved the bag down and sat up. She could hear her father's wheezing like it was in her bones. "What time is it?"

"Two. I've just put more logs on the fire. I should be back in an hour or so."

"Where's Mom?"

"Packing a bag. I've got the truck warming up." He handed her an alarm clock. "I've set this for four. If I'm not back, stoke the fire."

"I'm ready, David." Marge pulled on her coat. She handed him the suitcase. "Why don't you take this out first."

"What can I do?" Trish crawled out of her sleeping bag.

"Pray for us, for a safe trip on all that ice." Marge gave her a quick hug. "And for your dad."

With the recliner levered upright, it still took both Marge and David to get Hal to his feet.

With both of them supporting him, Trish wrapped the long wool scarf around his neck. She gave him a two-arm hug around the waist and after kissing his cheek, secured the scarf over his mouth and nose. "I love you." She bit back the tears that stung her eyes. "Come home quick."

Trish watched from the door as the three carefully made their way down the steps and navigated the sidewalk. Without the yardlight, she could only see them in the lights of the truck. David opened the door, and they boosted Hal in and placed the portable oxygen tank at his feet. Marge tucked a quilt around him and climbed in.

Trish kept watch until the red tail lights turned in the direction of town. Caesar whined at her feet. "Come on in." She slapped her leg. "You can keep me company."

The room seemed huge with everyone gone. She blew out one lamp and climbed back into her sleeping bag. The sofa would be more comfortable but the bag was closer to the fire. Caesar stretched himself beside her, his head on the sleeping bag, assuring Trish she was not alone.

"I don't know, old boy," she whispered. "I just don't know."

All she could think was *Please, please, please take care of my dad.* As she finally drifted off to sleep, their theme song floated through her mind. *Ah, yes, eagle's wings. You promised eagle's wings. And my dad really needs them—right now.*

David hadn't returned by the time the alarm went off. Bleary-eyed, Trish poked the remaining coals with the iron log turner and laid a small chunk of wood on the resurging flames. Eyes closed, she drowsed in front of the open doors. When the wood started to snap, she laid on two large chunks and crawled back into her sleeping bag.

The chill had already seeped back into the room so she shivered as she scrunched down and pulled the edge of the bag over her head. But the chill wasn't just in the room. The *please, please* rampaged through her head.

The wind whistled and groaned around the corners of the house, pleading at the windows for entry. Caesar snuggled closer. It felt like forever before Trish fell asleep again.

"You let the fire go out!" David's voice snatched away her sleepiness.

Trish sat up, but as soon as her nose felt the temperature of the room, she pulled her sleeping bag up with her. Daylight had lightened the room to gray. It was still early.

"How's Dad?"

"They're keeping him there." David knelt in front of the fireplace, poking and prodding the logs in search of live coals. "He was able to breathe better as soon as they gave him a shot. There." A small flame flared around the edges of the crumbling log. He added some kindling from the basket and a couple of small pieces of cedar.

Trish wrinkled her nose as a puff of wind blew smoke out into the room. "Did they say what was wrong?"

"They think bronchitis, maybe pneumonia again. Anyway, he's better off there where he can stay warm and eat right. I take it the lights haven't come back on?"

Trish shrugged. "The heat didn't, so I guess not."

"Well, let's get going. I stopped for water so we can get the chores done. Then I've gotta get the new generator and see how badly we're frozen up." David leaned his forehead on his fist as he sat on the hearth. His shoulders slumped. When Caesar shoved his nose into the other hand, David stroked the dog's head. It was an automatic reaction, but Trish could tell her brother was far away in his mind.

"David?" When there was no answer, Trish disengaged herself from the sleeping bag and reached up to touch his hand. "Is Dad worse than you're telling me?"

"Yes. No. I don't know. He's so sick again. It just

doesn't look good." David swallowed and rubbed his eyes. He turned to poke the fire one more time. As the flames danced higher, they glinted on a tear at the corner of his eye. He pushed himself to his feet.

"Come on, Caesar, time for you to go outside. Hustle, Tee." He let the dog out then headed down the hall to the bathroom.

Trish wrapped both arms around her legs and rested her chin on her knees. *Dad's gotta get better. Please God, he's gotta get well. I need my dad!* She stared into the flames, scenes from the last few days fast-forwarding through her mind. The Christmas Eve service, opening presents Christmas morning, her dad sick from the treatment, the sound of his fight to breathe.

"No! He's going to get well again. Heavenly Father, please." She rubbed her eyes hard with her fists. "This is no different than any other time he's been in the hospital. All I have to do is keep on going."

And keep on praying, her little voice reminded her.

How are we ever gonna do it all? Trish wondered as she pulled on her cold jeans and sweater. She'd slept in her long johns and wool socks to make dressing easier. When would she get to wash her hair again? she wondered. Or take a shower? When would they *finally* have electricity again?

She turned on the portable radio. "*. . . still have power outages over much of North Portland and Clark County. Crews are working around the clock to restore power.*"

"Tell me something I didn't know."

"*Some schools are open for emergency housing for those that need assistance.*" A list of schools followed.

"Well, at least I could go for a shower." Trish tugged on her boots.

"But people are encouraged to stay off the roads. Only drive if it is an absolute necessity."

"My hair is becoming a necessity."

"How about filling the teakettle before you leave?" David strode through the living room and out the door.

"Do you mind if I go to the bathroom first?" Trish grumbled. "And maybe brush my teeth?"

Only the wind answered her and its whine made her want to crawl back into the sleeping bag.

By the time the animals were fed and watered, Trish was more than ready to return to the house. Her nose felt about frozen off. She carefully checked the mare that was due to foal. They'd moved her into the big box-stall when the weather turned bad. The mare attacked her feed and drank deeply when Trish filled the bucket.

"Good girl," Trish stroked down the horse's neck and over her belly. Right in front of the mare's warm flank, Trish felt the foal kick. She held her hand firm but didn't feel it again. "Impatient aren't you, little one?" She could feel the grin that creased her face. What a thrill to feel that yet-to-be-born life. "But you take your time, you hear? You're not due for another ten days, so hang in there." She patted the mare once more and left the stall.

She gave Miss Tee and her mother extra grain for a treat and hugged the little filly close. Miss Tee sniffed Trish's face and whiskered her cheek. "I'll be back to clean your stall." Trish stroked the satiny nose and tickled the whiskery place on the filly's muzzle. "You be good."

Miss Tee nodded. Her tiny ears pricked forward as she watched Trish latch the stall door. A baby nicker followed Trish out the door. The nicker was much friendlier than the biting wind.

As soon as they had eaten their cereal, David left for Battle Ground to pick up a generator at the Co-op. Just as Trish was getting into her coat, the phone rang.

"Hallelujah!" Trish bounded into the kitchen. "Runnin' On Farm."

"Hi, Trish."

"Brad, what's happening? . . . You too, huh? We figured that when you didn't show up yesterday."

"What's going on there?"

Trish caught Brad up on the events of the previous day and night. "So how about I call you when David gets back. That is, if you're sure you can come help."

"I'll be over in a few minutes. Except for no power, everything's okay here."

Trish hung up the phone, a warm, fuzzy feeling in her midsection. It sure was good to have friends who just volunteered when you needed help.

She had four horses clipped to the hot walker by the time Brad got down to the stable. "Shoulda just walked," Brad said as he grabbed a pitchfork. "Almost ended up in the ditch turning into your driveway. I've never seen the roads like this."

"Yeah, David said it was bad, and he has chains and weight in the back of the pick-up."

"You aren't going to work any of them, are you?"

"No. Just the hot walker. If it warms up some, I think I'll let them out in the pasture." Trish pitched straw and manure out the stall door as she talked. Steam rose from the pungent pile.

Caesar's barking drew her attention to the house. Two camper pick-ups were following David up the driveway. "Who do you suppose that is?"

CHAPTER 8

Curiosity may have killed the cat but it made Trish stick her fork in the manure pile and trot up to the pump house where all three vehicles had parked.

As David climbed from the cab of the farm pick-up, four people slammed doors on theirs.

"We heard you needed help," a burly man tipped his hat back and extended his hand.

"Mr. Benson, Fred," David shook hands with the four guests. "How did you . . . I mean . . . why are. . . ?"

"Don't be surprised, son," Frank Johnson said. "Pastor called and when he told me your situation, why I figured you could use some extra hands. And places to heat water so we can thaw those pipes out." He pointed to the campers. "You know your dad's always been the first to help when needed, so we'd kinda like to pay him back."

"You don't mind, do you?" Benson asked.

"Why no, I . . ."

Trish could tell David was embarrassed as all get out. She blinked her eyes a couple of times. Who'd want frozen eyelashes?

"Good to see you, Trish." Frank Johnson smiled at her. "Hear you've been doing real well riding the ponies. We're real proud of you, you know. Just like one of our own kids, since we've known you all your growing-up years."

"Thank you." Trish could feel the blush staining her cheeks even redder than the cold had. "Well, uh, I've gotta get back to the barn. Thanks for coming." She hesitated only to watch two men pull the new red generator off the truck bed and carry it over to the pump house. "Wow! Who'd of thought today'd be like this?"

Well, you asked for help, didn't you? her nagger chuckled gleefully in her ear.

All the stalls were clean and horses groomed when one of the men came down to the barn. "We've got lunch up at the house. You hungry?"

Trish and Brad looked at each other. "Sure," she said.

"My wife figured you'd be about tired of hot dogs by now so she put a hot dish in the oven and salad in the fridge. Those campers come in handy when the power goes out."

Trish heard the chuckle in her ear again.

The women had even sent over paper plates and plastic forks. With the fire roaring in the fireplace and seven people laughing and talking, the house seemed almost like normal. Trish passed around the cake someone had sent for dessert and refilled coffee cups from a thermos. They'd thought of everything.

"Did you pick up the sleeping bags and stuff?" she asked David under cover of someone's joke.

"Yeah, when I came up to take care of the fire."

"Good," Trish breathed a sigh of relief. When she'd left the house the living room looked like a bunch of third graders had had a sleepover.

"Can you believe these guys? They've got the generator running and the pump thawed out. Now we've gotta find where the lines are frozen."

David seemed like a different person than the one Trish had known early that morning. She was glad to see the load lifted off his shoulders for a while.

When all the men went back to work, Trish carried the phone into the living room and closed the kitchen door again to keep the heat in. Holding the receiver to her ear was like wearing an ice pack. She dialed the hospital and asked for Hal Evanston's room.

"Where can they be?" she muttered after the third ring. "Come on, answer." After the sixth ring, the operator broke in.

"There doesn't seem to be any answer."

How'd you ever guess? Trish almost said aloud. Instead of screaming "Where's my dad?" like she wanted to, she bit her lip and said politely. "That's my father's room. Do you have any idea where he might be?" Her stomach clenched like it did just before the starting gate opened.

"Not for sure, but he could be down in X-ray. Can I leave him a message?"

"Please tell him or my mom that Trish called. We have a phone again but no lights yet. I'll call again later. Thank you." Trish clunked the phone back on the cradle. *What is going on there? Is Dad worse? Where's mother?*

Her thoughts still at the hospital, Trish went out to the back deck to bring in wood for the fireplace. She brought in three loads before brushing the bark and sawdust off her sweater. She was just closing the glass fireplace doors when the phone rang.

"Dad?" She clutched the receiver to her ear.

"No, silly. It's Rhonda. What's the matter?"

"Dad's back in the hospital, and when I called they

didn't know where he was." Trish slumped against the wall and slid to the floor.

"Oh, Trish, I didn't know."

"No one did. David took him in in the middle of the night. He looked awful when he left here. You know my dad. He had to work out in the cold to try to get the generator running. We don't have lights yet, and no water."

"We're basically in the same boat—we have water, but that's all. And a phone, as you can tell. Dad's gone on a business trip so Mom and I are kinda stuck here."

"Do you need anything?"

"No. Just company. This sure wasn't the way I planned to spend my vacation."

"Tell me about it. The only races I'm winning are with Caesar, and I don't tell him where the finish line is."

Rhonda chuckled.

"And if I don't get a shower pretty soon, no one will dare come near me."

"Gross. I know."

"Well, I gotta get back down to the barns and start the afternoon chores. Let me tell you about hauling water to all these animals. I don't think they ever drink this much. They just like to see me slave."

"Is Brad there?"

"Yeah, he came this morning. And there's some guys from church helping David with the pump and stuff."

"Say hi to everyone. Hey, Tee. You decided what to do for New Year's yet?"

Trish groaned. "Nope. Haven't even thought about it. Let's hope we're thawed out by then."

Hanging up, Trish debated whether to call the hospital again. Even while trying to talk herself out of it, her finger dialed the number. This time it was answered on the second ring.

"Mom?"

"Trish, oh, I'm so glad we have a phone again. What about the electricity?"

"Not yet. How's Dad?"

"Sleeping. We just got back from X-ray. And they've been giving him alcohol rubs to cool him off. We don't know a lot yet."

"Oh." Trish paused. "How did Pastor Ron know we needed help?"

"I called him this morning to have us put on the prayer chain again. Why?"

"Some men showed up to help. They even brought hot lunch in their campers. I couldn't believe it when I saw them drive in."

Trish could tell from the sniff she heard over the line that her mother had teared up. All of them seemed to be on the verge of bawling most of the time lately.

Marge blew her nose. "Tell them thank you from Dad and me. And Trish, call back this evening. I'm so worried about you two."

"You better worry more about Dad. We're okay. Brad is helping me and David expects to have water pretty soon. Love you." This time Trish set the phone down gently. The hospital seemed so far away.

As she stood up, she heard water running. She dashed into the bathroom. The toilet tank was filling. She checked the faucet. Water!

Then the kitchen. Not yet.

"No water in the kitchen," she hollered out the door. "But the bathroom works."

By the time she and Brad had finished the chores, the men had left. They had running water all the way to the barn and the house lines were clear. Thawing out the kitchen pipes had been the most difficult, she'd heard.

When Trish and Brad turned over the water tanks in the pastures after the cows and horses had a good drink, Trish said, "Maybe we can go skating tomorrow. Bet the pond is frozen solid by now."

Brad reached down and scratched Caesar's ruff. "I'll bring my skates. You need help with the chores in the morning?"

"Maybe. Ask David."

———

Trish didn't get a chance to talk to her dad before she crawled into her sleeping bag that night. He was sound asleep when she called. Her mother would stay the night in the hospital next to her husband.

David was snoring long before Trish could shut her mind off enough to even think about sleep. When she turned over and scrunched her pillow behind her head, she felt the bruise she'd gotten at the pump house. And her tailbone still hurt from the fall off the pick-up. But worst of all, her dad wasn't better. Some vacation.

The dim light of morning made the living room seem even colder. This time David had let the fire nearly go out. Trish turned her head. On the sofa David looked like a huge blue slug buried in his sleeping bag.

Trish stood up, keeping her bag around her. She sat on the hearth to poke the coals. When she saw a bit of red, she balled up newspaper and added it with a few small pieces of kindling. Finally she leaned forward and blew on it, trying to get a flame started.

"Come on, you," she both begged and ordered. When flames licked the wood, she added larger pieces and finally two small chunks. Trish watched as the fire grew, huddled in her sleeping bag and wishing for something hot for breakfast. Like her mother's fresh cinnamon rolls, or scrambled eggs or—

She waddled back to her mattress of quilts and lay down again. Maybe they could at least go out for lunch.

The phone woke them both sometime later.

David beat her to answer it. "Dad's a bit better," David said across the receiver. "Temperature's down." He listened again. "Mom wants to know if you want to come and shower there and stay for lunch."

Trish rolled her eyes heavenward. "Thank you, God, for small favors."

David smiled. "I think she said yes."

When Trish stepped outside, she could hardly believe her eyes. The sun had finally woken up and turned the ice to diamonds that dazzled everywhere—dangling from tree branches, icicles and fence posts. The "gems" glittered on bushes and sparkled off the pump house roof.

While the thermometer read only sixteen degrees, the sun would warm things up a bit. And better yet, the wind had died. Trish whistled, a sharp sound that brought an answer from the barn.

Trish skated her way down, deliberately choosing the icy patches to slide across. Arms waving, she almost took a tumble but righted herself. "No sense adding to my bruises," she informed a yipping Caesar. Spitfire progressed from a nicker to a full-blown whinny.

"All right, you guys, knock it off." Trish opened the top halves of stall doors as she made her way to the feed room. "You'd think I hadn't been down here in a week."

"Trish, come here!" David hollered from beyond the barn where he'd taken the truck to deliver water to the field stock.

"Now what?" She dropped the handles of the wheelbarrow and dashed around the corner. At the cow tank, David waved her on.

"Oh, wow!" Trish stopped at the fence. A fountain of ice hid the trough, turning a fir tree into a free-form statue. A broken waterpipe had shot water into the freezing air, sculpting the glistening work of art.

"Well, at least I know where this pipe's frozen." David shook his head. "Better drag another trough down here. Why don't you go up and get the camera. Dad'll enjoy seeing this."

After the chores were done, Trish packed clean clothes and shampoo into her sports bag.

"You better bring towels too," David reminded her. "I don't think the hospital is planning on us."

Once they reached Fourth Plain Boulevard, the road was clear.

"I shoulda taken the chains off," David grimaced at the clackety-clack in the wheel wells. "When we get there, you go on up and I'll take them off."

Trish didn't mind being the first to shower, but the old panic tried to strangle her as she inhaled the hospital odor at the front door. She swallowed hard and took the elevator to the third floor.

Hal was asleep when she tiptoed into the room. Marge put down her knitting and rose to give Trish a hug. "You look as bright as that sun out there." She hugged Trish again. "Hal, wake up. The kids are here."

Trish picked up her father's hand. "Dad, can you hear me?"

Hal's eyes fluttered open. He squeezed Trish's hand lightly, a good sign. "Hi, Tee." His voice seemed lost in the beep and whistle of the tubes and machines surrounding him. A slight lift of one side of his mouth could have been a smile.

Trish wheeled on her mother, and mouthed the words, "Is he going to die?"

CHAPTER 9

"No, Trish. Actually he's better."

"He doesn't look it." Trish stroked the back of her father's hand with her thumb.

"I know. But he could be a lot worse." Marge rubbed the back of her neck with one hand. "Where's David?"

"He decided to take the chains off." Trish could hardly get the words past the lump in her throat. She wanted to fling herself across her father's chest and plead with him to wake up. To smile at her and tell her everything would be all right. To get up out of that bed and go home.

She tried to hold it back, but one tear escaped and rolled down her cheek. *Come on, Dad. Wake up! See, I'm here to take a shower. You have no idea how bad I need a shower.*

Hal squeezed her hand faintly, but Trish felt it. Clear to her bones she felt the love in that small squeeze.

"Guess I'll hit the shower before David gets up here." She stuck her head back out the bathroom door. "You sure they don't mind? About us using the shower, I mean."

Marge shook her head. "No. They all know how many are still without power and water."

When Trish stepped under the stinging hot spray she

felt the worries of the last few days slither off her shoulders and flow down the drain with the soapy water. She shampooed once and then lathered up again. The water beating down on her head and shoulders felt heavenly. Finally she turned her back to the spray and let it pound on her upper back.

A knock sounded on the door. "You gonna take all day?" David sounded more than just a bit grumpy.

Trish turned to let the water stream over her face again, then shut off the spray. She wrapped one towel around her hair and dried off quickly with another. She looked with distaste at her clean long johns but put them on anyway. It would be time for chores when they got home and getting colder again.

Dressed in a plaid shirt and jeans, with a towel still around her head, she popped out the door. "Your turn, Davey boy." She grinned at him. "And take your time."

"Feel better?" The rasp in her father's voice told of the effort it took for him to speak.

Trish dropped her boots by the chair and whirled to his bedside. "Now I do." Her grin brightened the entire room. "Amazing how good a shower can feel. I'll never take hot water for granted again."

Hal's smile made it to his eyes this time.

"Everything's pretty good at home." By the time she'd told him about the ice sculpture, his eyes had drifted closed again. But his hand still clenched hers.

When she felt his hand relax, Trish dropped into the chair to pull on her boots. She rubbed most of the moisture out of her hair, then brushed and combed it into some semblance of style. After stretching both arms above her head, she dropped them to the floor and finally wrapped them behind her legs and pulled so her forehead rested on her knees.

"Oh, to be able to do that again," Marge said.

Trish stood upright and shook out her shoulders. "I haven't taken the time to stret lately. I'm really tight."

"Couldn't be because you've had anything else to do, could it?"

"Yeah, we've just been sittin' around." Trish wrapped both arms around her shoulders and pulled, rounding the kinks out of her upper back. "David gonna take forever? I'm starved."

"Look who's talking."

Trish heard the blow dryer in the bathroom. It wouldn't be long now.

A short time later they filed through the hospital cafeteria line. Trish felt like having one of everything. From the looks of David's tray, she was sure he had. "You gonna eat *all* that?" She stared at him in mock surprise.

"Just watch me."

God, let there be lights, she pleaded as they neared the farm drive a while later. But when Trish opened the sliding glass door, it didn't take a genius to know that her prayer hadn't been answered yet. Even the living room was cold because the fire had gone out. *Back to the real world.* She sighed at the mess scattered about; sleeping bags, blankets, clothes, dishes. *Well, at least we have running water. Even if it is cold.*

While David started the fire again, Trish picked things up and put them away. She stacked the bedding by the sofa. "How come this house feels so empty when Mom and Dad aren't here?"

David shrugged. "Beats me."

Another night without lights. The next morning the battery operated radio promised a warming by the afternoon. And the weather delivered. A chinook wind followed the sun and soon everything was dripping. The eaves, the trees, the frozen layer on top of the snow dribbled away. By the time the sun fell and took the temperature with it, Trish felt like spring had come.

When they walked into the house, the warmth hit their faces, and Trish could hear the familiar hum of the refrigerator.

"No hot dogs tonight!" Trish shouted, whirling down the hall to her bedroom. "And I get to sleep in my own bed!" She flopped back across it. "Fantastic!"

She could hear David in the kitchen listening to the answering machine.

"Call Rhonda," he told her when she entered the living room. "Maybe she'd like to work horses with you tomorrow."

"And maybe we'll have time to go skating. The ice won't melt that fast." Trish and Rhonda talked for half an hour.

" 'Bout time," David shook his head when she finally hung up the receiver. "Who ya calling now?"

"Brad. To remind him to bring his skates. We're going to have some fun for a change."

It was noon before the temperature rose above freezing, but not for lack of effort by the sun. The world glittered everywhere.

Trish hooked Gatesby to the hot walker while she rode Final Command. As Brad and David worked their way down the stalls, the piles of manure and straw grew, flavoring the air. Trish could hear them teasing each other as she walked the gelding back from the track.

"Who's next?"

"Let's do Gatesby. I want to enjoy the afternoon."

"Sorry I'm late." Rhonda trotted down the rise.

"Dad's coming home tonight, so Mom had all kinds of extra stuff for me to do. D'you think he ever notices that all the furniture has *just* been polished? Or that the shower was scrubbed? All he cares about is Mom's home cookin'.'"

"So she's doing some baking?"

"Yep. And I brought you all some." Rhonda pulled a packet of caramel rolls from inside her jacket. "I even kept them warm for you."

Trish pushed her horse's nose away when he tried to take a bite of her roll. "No way. This is for me."

"Tell your mom thanks." David wiped his mouth. "That was great."

"Sure." Rhonda smiled. "Okay, who we doing next?"

"You take Firefly and I'll do Gatesby. Then we can finish with Spitfire and Dan'l." Trish talked while she stripped the saddle off Final Command and slung it over the door. She ran a hand over his chest and down his front leg. "He's not even warm." She patted the sorrel neck. "Are you, fella? If only that next joker were as easy as you."

Gatesby rolled his eyes when she unclipped him from the hot walker. "Just be cool!" Trish ordered with a snap of the lead. She led him back to the stall and cross-tied him for good measure. Even so, she was quick on the sidestep when his ears went back and his bared teeth reached for her shoulder.

When she had him saddled and bridled, she unsnapped the leads and led him out by the reins, her hand clamped right beneath his chin.

"Watch him." She let David take her place at the head. Brad cupped his hands to boost her up. Just as she started to spring up, the horse scrambled to the side.

Trish floundered for her footing.

"You—" She couldn't think of a name to call him.

Gatesby perked his ears and looked around at her as if he wondered what could be the matter.

"Now stand still. You know better than that." This time when Brad boosted her, Trish landed in the saddle. She gathered her reins and settled her feet in the stirrups.

"Okay?" Brad looked up at her, concern in his eyes. "Maybe you should ride Dan'l and lead this clown."

"No. We'll be fine. He just needs a good workout. You ready, Rhonda?"

"Thanks, David." After the leg up, Rhonda settled her helmet in place and picked up her reins. "Maybe Brad's right."

For an answer, Trish nudged Gatesby forward. He walked flatfooted toward the track. "See, he's already gotten rid of all his meanness."

Trish kept a close eye on Gatesby's ears as they walked halfway around the track and then slow-jogged two more laps. Both horses snorted at the snow a couple of times.

Once Firefly crowhopped. Rhonda clamped her knees and laughed as she pulled the filly back down. "Thought you'd get away with something, didn't you?"

Gatesby twitched his ears and shook his head.

"How's your dad?" Rhonda kept Firefly even with Trish's mount.

"Mom says he's better but I can't tell. He can hardly talk on the phone." Trish glanced over at Rhonda. "Let's gallop but keep it slow."

Gatesby tugged at the bit but settled into a steady pace at Trish's command. The two horses matched stride for stride.

Trish let him out a bit and glanced over her shoulder at Rhonda.

With a loud whoosh, snow cascaded off a nearby fir tree and thumped to the ground.

Gatesby exploded. He leaped forward; his front feet slid in a patch of snowy mud. As he went down to his knees, Trish felt herself flying through the air.

A loud crack shattered the stillness as the top fence board crashed beneath her weight.

CHAPTER 10

Trish struggled to her feet.

"Are you all right?" Rhonda leaped off Firefly, and dragging the filly behind her, ran to her fallen friend. "Trish, are you hurt?"

Trish shook her head and blinked her eyes. "Just the breath knocked out of me, I think."

"There's blood on your face. You've been cut."

"I'm okay." Trish felt like she was talking through a tunnel. "How's Gatesby?" She leaned against the fence post she'd just missed in her flight.

Rhonda looked around. "He must have gone back to the barn. You want me to get David?"

"No! I'm okay. I'll—" Trish took one step and the pain blasted from her arm to her brain. "Yeah, you better get David. Tell him to bring the truck." Rhonda was on Firefly and off before Trish knew what was happening.

Trish blinked against the shock. She looked down. Her right arm dangled at her side. She could feel warm liquid oozing down her wrist. When she tried to raise the arm, she bit back the scream that ripped clear up from her toes. A deep breath to clear her mind knifed another pain through her side and chest.

She tried to concentrate on the ground in front of her. The sun that had been so welcome now blinded her, re-

91

flecting off the snow and ice.

You're not going to faint! she commanded herself. She shifted her feet. Agony thundered through her body and left her breathless. *Take a deep breath.* The side pain struck again. *Dumb idea!*

Brad leaped out of the truck before it stopped moving. "Trish! Trish! Oh, no!"

She tried to smile around her gritted teeth. "It's both my arm and my side. You better get me to the hospital—quick."

"Call 911," David told Brad, trying to remain calm. "Trish, there's blood soaking your sleeve."

Brad jumped back in the truck and gunned it. Mud and slush sprayed up from the back wheels.

"I know. Remember where the upper arm pressure point is?" She swallowed the bitter taste at the back of her throat. "We're going to put our first-aid class to work." She spoke each word slowly, separately, as if hearing herself from a distance.

"Remember? Right above the elbow." She ground her teeth against the pain when David touched her arm. "Careful!"

"I can't, Trish!"

"Yes, you can. Just pinch it hard." She felt her knees begin to sag. She clutched the post with her left arm. "Can you feel the pulse?"

"Yes." David clamped his fingers around her upper arm. He wrapped his other arm around her so she could lean against him. "Would you be better off sitting down?"

Trish shook her head. "Is Rhonda taking care of the horses?"

"Yes."

Trish leaned her head on David's chest. Between his arms and the fence she felt secure.

"Maybe we could just go in ourselves. Do you think we could make it?"

"Tri-ish. How would I get you into the pick-up?"

"Just toss me in." The fog seemed to be rolling in—everything looked hazy. "You know, like a bale of hay or a sack of feed."

The truck plowed to a stop in front of them and Brad leaped out. "Here, I grabbed some blankets and a sleeping bag. If she goes into shock, we're in real trouble."

"We're in . . . real . . . trouble . . . now," Trish murmured.

"Lay that sleeping bag out and then help me get her down," David instructed. "I can't let go of her arm."

Trish could hear David talking ever so faintly. The fog rolled in and out. "No-o-o!" She moaned as Brad lifted her as carefully as possible, and with David bracing her arm, laid her on the sleeping bag and covered her with the other blankets.

The siren wailed in the distance.

"Rhonda'll show 'em where we are," she heard Brad say.

"Mom's . . . really . . . gonna be mad." The pain wasn't so bad if she didn't move.

David knelt beside his sister, his fingers locked on the pressure point. "Don't worry about that."

"Mm-mmm."

They cut the siren and the ambulance pulled up beside the threesome. Trish could hear doors slamming and then a woman's smiling face was close to hers.

"Decided to take a tumble, eh?" The voice matched the smile.

"Okay, son." A man's voice carried the same degree of comfort. "You can let go of her arm now."

"My ribs too—I think." Trish barely lifted her head to see what they were doing.

"Just take it easy, Trish. I'm going to cut this sleeve off so we can look at that arm." The pain changed from pulsing to piercing. "Compound fracture of the right radial," he spoke to the woman jotting down the diagnosis. "Bleeding is slowing, we'll splint and bandage."

"Here," the woman slipped a length of tubing around Trish's head and adjusted the prongs in her nose. "A little oxygen is going to make this next part a bit easier for you."

Trish gritted her teeth so hard she thought her jaw would break. She wasn't sure whether it was tears or perspiration running into her ear.

When the arm was stabilized the medic said to her, "Now, you mentioned your ribs. Right side?"

Trish nodded. The lightest touch made her clench up again.

"Okay, let's get you on a board and brace your neck."

"Why? That doesn't hurt." Trish was puzzled.

"You've had what is called an ejection trauma. There could be spinal damage. We've got to take precautions. You don't mind do you?"

Trish nodded.

With efficiency and precision the two picked up the corners of the sleeping bag, and hoisted her onto a wheeled gurney.

"I'll follow you in the truck," David told her.

"Sorry we can't go skating," Trish said when Rhonda leaned over the gurney.

Rhonda bit her lip. "Just take it easy, buddy. We'll go

skating another time." She patted Trish's good hand. "See you there."

"Rhonda," Trish called just above a whisper. "How's Gatesby?"

"Ornery as ever, and my shoulder will be fine after a week or two."

Trish smiled at her. "Thanks."

"Ready?" the woman asked.

Trish nodded and they slid the whole contraption into the ambulance.

"Okay," the woman spoke again. "I'm going to start an IV before we get rolling, so you'll feel another prick." She tied a rubber strap around Trish's left arm. "How about a fist now? There, you're an easy one." She taped the needle and tubing in place and started the drip. "Okay, let's roll."

No matter how carefully they drove, every movement vibrated in Trish's arm. The bumps in the road, slowing at intersections, then rolling the stretcher out at the hospital. Trish nearly fainted when they transferred her to an examining table in the emergency room.

She kept her eyes half closed to fade out the bright lights overhead.

"I'm going to get the rest of your clothes off," a nurse spoke as she began removing Trish's jeans before she could respond.

"It's a bad break, isn't it?" Trish forced herself to ask.

"Yeah, honey, you did it up royal this time." The nurse smiled down at her. "But don't you worry, we're gonna fix you up just fine."

Trish smiled back at the friendly dark face.

"Your mom's here." The nurse stepped back as Marge entered the room.

"I always knew I'd find you in the emergency ward someday." Marge kissed Trish on the forehead. She looked at the nurse. "How bad is she?"

A man brusquely entered the room. "Once we take care of that arm, she'll be fine. I'm Doctor Burnaby, and we've called in an orthopedic surgeon. We'll get some X-rays, then as soon as we get the operating room ready, we'll be on our way." He stepped to the head of the gurney and spoke to Trish, "How's that sound to you, young lady?"

Trish tried to smile around her tears.

Flat on her back, the hospital took on a strange appearance for Trish. All she could really see were the ceiling tiles as they pushed the gurney through the halls.

When they entered another brightly lit room, they transferred her to another hard surface.

A man dressed in baggy green clothes took her hand. "I'm Dr. Johanson, your anesthesiologist. We're going to put you to sleep for a while, Trish. And when you wake up, your mother will be right here, okay?"

Trish nodded. *Do I have a choice?*

———————

"Hi, there."

Trish wished the voice would go away and let her sleep.

"Do you know what your name is?"

Trish forced her eyes open. "Tricia . . . Evanston." Her mouth felt like it was full of cotton. It hurt to swallow. "Can I have a drink?"

"Not yet, but here's an ice chip to suck on."

The bit of liquid helped. Trish fell back into the chasm she'd been drifting in.

———————

"Welcome back," Marge smoothed the hair back from Trish's brow.

"Hi, Mom." Trish blinked her eyes open. This time the weights weren't so heavy. And the light didn't blind her.

Marge held a straw to Trish's mouth. "I think a drink will make you feel lots better."

Trish nodded as she sucked on the straw. "How come my throat is so dry?"

"From the anesthetic and the tube they put down your throat during surgery."

"How's my arm?"

"They had to pin and plate the bones back together. You have stitches where the broken bone pierced your arm and where they put the pin in."

Trish thought a moment. "That's why I was bleeding, huh?"

"Yes. You cracked a couple of ribs too, so you probably won't want to laugh much for a while. Oh, and they put two stitches in that cut on your chin."

"How come I'm so cold?"

"Could be that ice pack around the cast on your arm. Here, let me put another pillow under it so you won't feel the cold so much. And I'll get another blanket."

Trish felt her eyes drooping again. "Won't be riding for a while, right?"

"Right." Marge patted her daughter's cheek. "You sleep and I'll go tell your dad how you're doing. I love you, Trish."

Trish smiled. "Me, too. Tell Dad I'm okay." She didn't even hear her mother close the door.

The next twenty-four hours passed in a blur of pain, sleep, ice, faces coming and going—and thirst.

"Trish, you have company," she heard her mother's voice as if in the distance.

She blinked till she could see Rhonda, Brad and David surrounding her bed. "Hi, guys."

Marge placed the straw in Trish's mouth again and she drank deeply.

"Boy, you sure scared us." Rhonda shook her head.

"Me, too."

"We brought you something." Brad set a ceramic horse planter on her bedside table. Three helium balloons were tethered to the horse's neck with bright ribbons. Red carnations dominated the variety of plants in the planter.

"That's really cool. Thanks." Trish turned her head to look. "Mom, how do I make this bed go up, so I can see better?"

Marge pushed the button clipped to the sheet beside Trish's head. "Let's dangle this thing over the rail so you can see where it is."

Trish winced as the rising bed shifted her arm and ribs. "Guess I won't be running any races for a few days."

"Yeah, you were kinda hard on the fence, too." David tapped her toe.

"How's Gatesby?"

"Sore, but he'll live to bite again."

"He already has." Brad rubbed his arm.

Trish started to laugh at the pained look on his face, but immediately decided a smile would do. "Please don't make me laugh. It hurts."

"Can I bring you anything else?" Rhonda asked when they got ready to leave a few minutes later.

"I'll call you if I think of anything. Thanks for coming." Trish pushed the button to lower her bed again. "Mom, when can I go see Dad?"

"I don't know. We'll ask the doctor when he comes in."

"They oughta put Dad and me in the same room. It would be easier for you." Trish felt her eyelids drooping again.

"Good idea. I'll be sure to ask. If I'm not here when you wake up, you know where I'll be."

Trish and her father went home together on January second.

"At last," Marge sighed as she leaned back in her rocker after everyone was settled. Trish lay back in the recliner. Hal was sound asleep in his bed. "What a way to start the New Year."

"Mm-mmm." Trish scratched her scalp. Her arm itched too, under the cast that extended from her upper arm to the palm of her hand. "Mom, how am I gonna manage at school?"

"It won't be easy. How are you at writing with your left hand?"

"Lousy. You saw how I did at eating." Trish wriggled her toes in her slippers. "And I haven't even tried to put real clothes on yet."

"We'll just have to take one day at a time. The doctor said it would be at least a week at home. Maybe I should go buy you a couple of sets of sweats. They'd be comfortable and you could use the bathroom by yourself."

Trish groaned. "I hadn't even thought about that."

"What color would you like? I'll get extra large tops

so you can get them on easily and have plenty of room for the cast and sling."

"And I'll look like a dork."

"Mmm. Whatever that is. Why don't we go to the hairdresser tomorrow and get your hair washed. It would be a lot easier than the kitchen sink."

"Do people really live for six weeks without showers?"

"I'm sure they do."

———

One week later Trish stared into the dancing flames lapping at the logs in the fireplace. This had to go down as the worst Christmas vacation in history.

Two mornings later Trish stared in the mirror. *Good thing I don't wear a lot of makeup. I can't see myself putting mascara on with my left hand.* Her new forest green sweats made her look like a jock. *Maybe I'll start a new fad—the one-arm look.* The sling held the cast close to her body, and Marge had tucked the right sleeve into the armhole so it wouldn't get in her way.

"Come on, Trish, you're going to be late." David had just come up from the barn. "I'll take you."

"You going to be okay?" Rhonda asked when they met in front of their lockers.

"I've got to be." Trish leaned her forehead against her locker. "Rhonda, I never dreamed anything could be so hard. Having only one good arm is the pits."

At noon Trish called for her mother to come and get her. "I hurt so bad." She bit back the sobs; they only made her ribs hurt worse.

CHAPTER 11

"You're late again."

Trish slammed her hair brush into the sink. It bounced out, knocking a glass bottle of hand lotion into the sink. It sounded like the entire medicine cabinet had come crashing down.

"What on earth? Trish, are you all right?" Marge tried to open the door. It was locked. "Trish?"

Trish propped her weight on her good arm and stared at the sink. "I—I'm fine, Mom." At least the bottle hadn't broken, but it *had* chipped a piece out of the sink enamel. She turned to unlock the door. Tears puddled in her eyes and ran down her cheeks. *Everything is so unfair!*

When Trish opened the door, she was looking straight at her mother. Trish sniffed.

"Can we talk about it?"

"No, I'm late. I'm always late because everything takes twice as long. Getting dressed, combing my hair, brushing my teeth. I couldn't even get the cap back on the toothpaste because I was dressed, and my arm was under my sweatshirt." Trish paused to blow her nose. "I can't even blow my nose right."

Marge followed Trish to her bedroom.

"And when I get to school, I can't open the door if I have books in my arm. I'm sick and tired of asking people to help me!" She dropped to the edge of her bed.

"Anything else?"

"Yes! It's been three weeks since I've ridden and the doctor said it'll be another three."

"Actually, I think you've done pretty well."

Trish glared up at her mother. "Right!"

"Trish, I know it's hard, but let's not fight about it." She handed her a tissue. "Here, I'll go write an excuse."

"Can't I just stay home?" Trish knew her question would be ignored.

You don't really want to stay home, her little voice whispered. *Remember how bored you got the week before you could go back to school?*

Trish stuffed her books into her bag, slung it over her shoulder and grabbed her jacket with one finger. Marge helped her put it on. Trish slumped in the passenger's seat. *I wish I could at least drive!*

It had been a miserable three weeks. At first all she wanted to do was sleep because of the pain—then the boredom. She felt terrible, she looked terrible, and everything seemed too difficult—too hard to bother doing. At least if she stayed in her room she didn't have to impress anyone.

She tried to put on a good front at school, even managed to laugh sometimes. But it felt as if heavy plaster casts were stacked on her shoulders—like the one on her arm. Her arm still ached at times, especially by the end of the day. All she wanted to do when she got home was go to sleep.

"You comin' down to the stables to watch us work the horses?" Brad asked on the way home.

"No."

"But, Trish, it's about time—"

"I said no."

Rhonda leaned forward on the back of the car seat. "Maybe watching training would cheer you up, make you feel better."

"Thank you, Dr. Shrink." Trish gritted her teeth. "Just don't get on my case, okay?"

The remainder of the drive was silent.

Saturday Firefly was scheduled to run in the fourth race and Final Command in the seventh. Genie Stokes had worked both of them and would ride in the races.

"Aren't you ready yet?" Hal asked after lunch. This would be his first time back at the track since Christmas. "I'm really looking forward to the races. See, the sun even came out just for us."

"That's nice. But I've got homework to do," Trish managed. "It takes me forever to write a paper, you know."

"Trish, go get ready," her father said sternly.

"No thanks." She left the table and headed for her bedroom.

Hal found her lying on her bed, staring at the wall. "I'm asking you to get ready and go with me."

"Please." Trish covered her eyes with the back of her hand. "I really don't feel up to going."

"All right. But this has gone on long enough, Tee. You and I are going to have to talk tonight."

Hal was worn out when he came home and went straight to bed.

I didn't think he was strong enough to spend all that time at the track, Trish thought indignantly.

At least he tried. Her nagger was becoming a permanent resident in her ear. *You've been—*

"Just be quiet!" Trish ordered. She flexed the fingers

of her left hand to ease a cramp before picking up her pen again to finish her paper. It took real effort to form some of the letters. *Well, at least I can use White-Out. It's better than throwing a page away and starting over.* She blocked out the words that looked too bad and blew on the white liquid until it was dry. One thing she'd found handy was to fasten her paper to a clipboard. That way it didn't scoot all over when she tried to write.

Trish went to church the next morning under much duress. From the looks on her parents' faces when she asked to stay home, she didn't dare ask again. *But I don't have to listen,* she promised herself. *I don't think God cares anymore, so why should I?*

Everyone was happy to see Hal back. They reminded him of their prayers for him as well as for Trish. Gritting her teeth was getting to be a necessary habit. She got so weary of saying "I'm fine" when people asked "How are you?" that she went to sit in the car. *I should tell them how I really feel.* Her thoughts continued in a negative vein.

You want to know what I think? her nagger chimed in.

"No. Not really." Trish slumped lower in the seat.

I think you're just throwing a pity party—poor Trish.

"Easy for you to say." Trish wished she could put her hands over her ears in an attempt to drown him out.

"Stay in the car," Hal told Trish when they arrived home. "You and I are going for a drive."

"I—uh—I have to use the bathroom," Trish scrambled for a way out.

"Okay. I'll wait for you here." Hal settled himself behind the wheel. "Why don't you bring a couple of your mother's fresh cinnamon rolls? That should hold us till dinner."

"We'll be ready to eat about three," Marge said before shutting the door.

"Now, where would you like to go?" Hal asked when Trish returned to the car. Her mother had had to push her out the door.

"I don't care." Trish struggled with the seat belt.

"How about Lake Merwin?"

Trish shrugged.

"Want a milkshake in Battle Ground?"

"Not really." She chewed her bottom lip. "But if you want one . . ."

Trish looked out the window without really seeing the scenery. What she *wanted* to do was take a nap. Life was so much simpler when she was sound asleep.

She felt the car come to a stop. When she opened her eyes she could see the blue lake glistening in the winter sun. Hundred-foot-tall fir trees sighed in the breeze. She examined her fingernails.

"You haven't been down to see the horses much lately." Hal turned in his seat and picked up a cinnamon roll. "They miss you."

"It's easier not to."

"That's not like you, to choose the easiest way." He waited for an answer. When Trish remained silent, he continued. "Why don't you tell me what's bothering you?"

Trish shrugged.

"You're not eating."

"Guess I'm not hungry."

"Come on, Tee. Let me in so I can help you."

"Isn't it obvious?" Trish angled her body to face him. "I can't ride. I can't write. I'm clumsy. And when I bang into things, I hurt. I'm tired all the time. I—" She drew circles on her pant leg with her fingernail.

"Yes?"

"I feel ugly and stupid and I'm sick and tired of these sweats and . . ." She sniffed the tears back. "And I *hate* blubbering all the time and . . ."

"And?" Hal's voice was soft, gentle, the voice he used around the horses so they wouldn't spook.

"And . . ." Trish swiped her hand across her eyes. Her voice dropped to a whisper. "I'm scared." She raised her gaze to meet her father's. "Dad, I'm so scared."

Hal reached over and closed his hand over hers. "Scared of what?"

"What if my arm doesn't get better before the Santa Anita trip? What if I can't race or even work Spitfire before then? He'll be out of condition and won't have a chance down there."

"Anything else?"

"And you were so sick. I thought for sure you were going to die." Tears brimmed over and ran down her cheeks.

"Trish, I didn't even come close to dying."

"But you were so weak."

"Yeah, infection and lack of oxygen do that to me. I did a stupid thing, working on the generator in that cold. I should have listened to your mother and just bought a new one in the first place. I'm really sorry I put you all through the extra worry just because of my pride. Will you forgive me?"

Trish stared at him. "But it's not your fault."

"Trish, we aren't responsible for the things that happen to us but we *are* responsible for the way we react to them. Take for instance, your broken arm. Now that was an accident, right?"

"Well, I should've been paying closer attention."

"Maybe. But we can *all* play the 'shoulda' game. It just doesn't get us anywhere. Just like I 'shoulda' stayed out of the cold. You can't change what has already happened."

Trish felt like one of the weights had been lifted from her shoulders.

"Now, about your arm healing. Is there any reason why it shouldn't heal?"

"No, I guess not."

"Have you been praying about it?"

She chewed her lip. "Sorta." She swallowed the word.

"Been a little bit mad at God, have you?"

"Well, if He won't help us, can't He at least just leave us alone?" The words spewed out, harsh and biting. "We pray and pray and still things go wrong. You're sick, I'm broken, the ice storm, the . . . the . . ." She huddled back in the corner by the door, appalled at what she'd said.

"Oh, Trish, I know things have been bad. But look at all the good things. Remember that blank book I gave you? One of the good things about a journal is that you can go back and read what you felt in both good times and bad. Jesus never promised us there wouldn't be any trouble, just that He'd carry us through it. I can't even begin to comprehend how bad things could be or might have been without Him."

Trish pointed to her casted arm. "I have enough trouble trying to keep up writing for school right now without adding another writing project."

"True, for now. But think with me of some good things."

Trish frowned. She licked her lips, stretched her

neck. "Uh-h-h, the snow and ice are gone."

"What else?"

"You're better. But now it's time for another treatment and you'll be sick all over again."

"Maybe. But not for long. Keep going."

"I'm learning to be ambidextrous." A grin tried to escape the corners of her mouth.

"True. Who knows when that could come in handy?"

"The eagle I gave you for Christmas."

"True. That's a symbol for all time."

Trish drew in a breath that went all the way to her toes. "I've been pretty awful, haven't I?"

"Let's just say I'm glad this side of you doesn't come out very often."

Trish leaned her head back on the seat. "At least Mom hasn't had to worry about my riding."

"I think at this point she'd rather be worrying about your racing than your depression."

"Really?"

"Really. And Tee, talking things over always makes you feel better. You don't have to carry the whole world by yourself." He started the car. "Let's go home for dinner."

David met them after they'd parked the car in front of the house. "The mare foaled sometime while we were gone. A colt, a real strong one."

"Come on, Trish. Let's go see him." Hal patted her hand. "And greet all your lonesome friends down at the barn."

The colt was nursing when they approached the stall. His tiny brush of a tail flicked back and forth while his mother watched the visitors carefully.

"He has four white socks and a diamond between his

eyes that doesn't quite make a blaze. There's another tiny diamond on his muzzle. Wait till you see his face." David leaned on the door next to his father and Trish.

"So what do we name him?" Trish rested her chin on her forearm against the stall door. "Star Bright? Diamond Dan? Uh-m-mm."

"How about Double Diamond?" Hal looked at them.

"I like that. Double Diamond to win. And the winner of this year's Kentucky Derby is Double Diamond, bred and owned by Hal Evanston and ridden by Tricia Evanston." Trish fell into the cadence of a race announcer.

"Sounds good." David nodded. He slid open the bolt on the door and took a bucket of warm water in for the mare. "Easy girl. You've done well."

Trish visited with each of her head-tossing, nickering and whuffling friends. Even Gatesby seemed glad to see her. He didn't try once to take a nip. Spitfire draped his head over Trish's good shoulder and closed his eyes in bliss as she scratched his cheek.

Miss Tee hung back until Trish opened the stall door and slipped inside. She extended a handful of grain, and after lipping that, the filly allowed Trish to cuddle her.

"She almost forgot me," Trish moaned they walked back up to the house. "Guess I better get down here every day."

―――――

The countdown till cast-off day began when Trish had two weeks left to go. Every morning she marked another square off on the calendar. And each day she reviewed the cards on her wall. Her father's latest addition was from Proverbs 17:22. "A cheerful heart is a good medicine."

Trish reminded herself of that one when she felt the weights try to pile up on her shoulders again.

"Tomorrow, tomorrow, I'll love you tomorrow," Trish couldn't stop singing. The cast would come off tomorrow. After the visit to the doctor's office, she would be able to wear *real* clothes again. And take a shower. No more washing her hair in the sink.

The next morning in the doctor's office, the buzzing of the saw sent shivers up and down her spine. *What if he slips and cuts my arm while cutting through the cast?*

"Don't worry, Trish. I haven't cut off any arms yet," the doctor said, reading her mind. He turned off the saw and separated the two pieces of the cast.

"Yuck!" Trish looked from the stark white arm up to her mother and back again. "It looks terrible!"

"Let's get that X-rayed," the doctor said, inspecting the incision. "Then we'll see what happens next."

Trish laid her arm on the X-ray table. She stared at the grungy line around her thumb and across her fingers where she hadn't been able to scrub. She really had a scar too, right along the top of her forearm.

"Okay." The technician pushed open the door. "Got some good ones. You can go back up to the doctor's office and wait for him to read them."

Trish slipped her arm back into the sling with Marge's help. Visions of riding again filled her mind as they waited for the elevator to reach the right floor. And tomorrow she'd wear the new sweater she'd gotten for Christmas. And jeans.

"I'm sorry, Trish." The doctor studied the X-ray. "We're going to have to cast you again. That bone just isn't strong enough yet to take a chance on it."

CHAPTER 12

"Another two weeks?"

"I'm sorry, Trish." The doctor did look sorry. "But if you broke it again now, it would be a lot more than two weeks. We have to make sure that bone is healed properly."

Trish gritted her teeth and rolled her eyes toward the ceiling to keep the tears from falling. *There goes the next race for Spitfire. That's next week.* Despair clogged her mind.

"You said *at least*. Does that mean it could be longer?" Trish looked the doctor full in the face.

"Let's hope not. I'll put the cast back on today and we'll schedule another appointment in two weeks."

Trish brightened. "Can I ride anyway? If I'm careful?"

The doctor thought a moment, then shook his head. "You'd be taking a pretty big chance. Better wait. The two weeks will go by quickly."

"I'm sorry, Trish," Marge said on the way home. "I know how much you were counting on having the cast off."

Trish let the tears run down her cheeks. She didn't try to fight them back; she didn't mop them up. It was just too much.

One look at her face when she walked through the door and Hal knew the verdict. He put both arms around her and asked over the top of her head, "How long?"

"Minimum of two weeks," Marge answered for her.

"Okay." He drew Trish over to the fireplace and sat beside her on the hearth. "I know this is throwing you right now, Tee, but here's what I suggest. I'll call Genie Stokes tonight and ask her if she can come out here tomorrow afternoon. We'll try her up on Spitfire with you standing there to help control him. Maybe he'll listen to you."

Trish leaned over and pulled a tissue from the box on the end table. She blew her nose, wiped her eyes, and tossed the tissue in the fireplace. With each movement, she sat straighter, shoulders back and head up.

She took a deep breath and paused for a moment, thankful deep breathing didn't hurt anymore. *After all, two weeks isn't forever. I made it this far, I can go the distance.*

"What if we hooded him?" She thought for a long moment about her idea, her chin resting in her hand. She'd braced her elbow on her knee. "Maybe he'll be okay if I lead him around for a while."

"That's my girl." Hal patted her knee.

Trish called Rhonda as soon as school was out. "Bad news, buddy," she said. "I'm recasted."

"Oh no-o-o." Rhonda's moan echoed through the receiver. "How could they?"

"Real easy. He just wrapped that gooey stuff round and round and said, 'See you in two weeks.' "

"Can you ride anyway?"

"No. I tried that idea out on him but no go. Rhonda, I was so mad I felt like punching him or something. He's ruining my life! At this rate, the racing season will be over before I get back up on a horse. We shoulda made you ride Spitfire all along so he would allow someone else on his back."

"What're you gonna do?"

"Well, I'm *not* going to take a nap! I've got horses to groom and a filly to train. And Double Diamond is almost as cute as Miss Tee. Come on over."

"Can't. I have horses to work too, you know."

"I know. Just had to give you my *wonderful* news. Yuck!" Trish hung up the phone. . . . *will raise you up on eagle's wings.* Like a melting snowbank, the song trickled through her mind. She stopped in front of the mantel in the living room and stroked the carved feathers on the eagle's wing.

"Thank you for the healing going on in my arm," she whispered in prayer that night. "And in my Dad." She thought a moment. "And in my mind. Amen!"

Genie Stokes drove in the drive right after Brad dropped Trish off the next afternoon. Genie opened her door and stepped out. "Tough luck, Trish. I sure know how you're feeling."

"Come on in. I don't know where Dad is, but Mom probably has the coffeepot on. How've you been doing?" Trish led the way up the walk.

"Not bad now that the weather's cleared up. We were all really sorry to hear about your accident. You never know what will happen next in this crazy business. Hi, Mrs. Evanston. Mm-mm, it smells wonderful in here."

"Hal and David will be right back. You've got time for a snack if you'd like. There's coffee, hot chocolate . . ."

"Diet Coke, juice." Trish dug caramel off the wax paper and stuck it in her mouth. "And cinnamon rolls."

Down at the barn half an hour later, David saddled Spitfire and held him for Genie to mount. Trish stood right beside the colt's head, scratching his ears and explaining what they were going to do.

Hal boosted Genie into the saddle.

Spitfire snorted. He laid his ears back.

"Easy, fella, you don't mind what we're doing," Trish consoled.

Spitfire threw his head up, ripping the reins from Trish's hand.

"Get back, Trish!" Hal barked the order.

"Spitfire, no!" Trish clamped her good hand over the horse's muzzle. The colt snorted. His eyes rolled white. He jerked his head back, forcing Trish to stumble to the side. She went down on one knee, still trying to calm the horse with her voice.

"Trish, Trish," Hal muttered as he lifted her to her feet.

When Spitfire's front feet left the ground, Genie vaulted lightly to the dirt.

"Let's try the hood." Trish turned to get her father's reaction.

"We'll try it, but I don't think it'll do any good." Hal shook his head. "I just can't take the chance on his injuring someone."

Trish soothed the trembling horse. "Come on, fella, no one's gonna hurt you. You know we wouldn't do that." She led him around in a circle until he rested his head on her shoulder.

He was worse with the hood in place. He lashed out with both front and back feet as soon as Genie settled in the saddle. Nothing Trish said or did made any difference.

"That's it," Hal said. "I'll scratch him. Thanks for trying, Genie."

"Don't worry, Tee," Hal said at dinner that night. "The forced rest won't hurt him any. We'll think about a race in early March, just depends."

Yeah, Trish thought. *Depends on how my arm does. Why didn't I have Rhonda ride him once in a while when we were training him? Then we wouldn't have this problem.*

The countdown to cast-off narrowed to three days, then two and finally it arrived. But this time Trish wasn't so confident. The doctor had said the two weeks was minimum.

"I'm scared," Trish told Rhonda and Brad in the lunchroom. "I can't stand the thought of more time in this thing." She thumped on the cast with her left hand. "What if. . . ?"

"Knock it off." Rhonda took another bite of her tuna sandwich. "This is the day. After 3:30 P.M. you will be a free woman."

"That's it! Rhonda has spoken." Brad patted her on the head as he stood to take his tray back. "Your mom picking you up?"

Trish nodded. "Sure hope you two are right."

They were. The X-rays showed the bone had mended.

Trish winced as the doctor cut off the cast. That whirling blade was awfully close to the skin on her arm.

"Now don't go falling off any more horses." The doctor grinned at her. "And take it easy on that arm for a while. You may still have occasional pain if you over-extend yourself." He handed her a red rubber ball. "Use this to rebuild those muscles. Just clench and release it. Start with about five at a time and work up."

"Thanks," Trish stuck her arm in the sleeve of her sweatshirt and zipped up her jacket with her right hand. She felt like she was floating out the door.

"You want to stop for a celebration sundae?" Marge asked as they got back in the car.

"Nope!" Trish shook her head emphatically. "I'm going home to take an hour-long shower and wash my own hair. Then I'll call Rhonda and tell her the good news."

Marge chuckled. "Hope the hot water lasts that long." They headed for home. "But remember, the doctor said to take it easy at first. I think that means no riding for a couple of days at least."

Trish refused to comment. Her mother's worrying would *not* take the spangle off this day.

The shower was everything she'd dreamed it would be. She stood with her back to the spray, enjoying the feel of hot water pounding on her neck and shoulders. She felt really clean for the first time in two months. When the water cooled, she turned off the tap and wrapped a towel around her head, drying off with another.

She could hardly find the mirror in the steamy bathroom, but she saw enough to compare her right arm to her left. It was definitely thinner. And all that dry, flaky skin? Yuck! She slathered on hand lotion, then studied the scar.

"Well, at least it'll shrink with time. And a suntan." She nodded at the grinning face in the mirror. "And *you* are going to California in five weeks—to get that suntan."

Back in her room she found she needed her left hand to snap the closure on her jeans. But now she had two hands that worked together to button her shirt and tie her shoes. She felt like cheering at the thought of being back in *real* clothes.

She squeezed on the red ball while she waited for Rhonda to answer the phone.

"Hello?"

Trish deepened her voice. "Rhonda Seaboldt, you're talking to a free woman. This prisoner has dropped her chains."

"All right!"

When they hung up half an hour later, Marge extended a hand to pull Trish up from her place on the floor, propped against the cabinets. "Well, free woman, how about setting the table? Your dad and David are on their way up."

"What smells so good?" Trish lifted the lid on a steaming kettle. "You made spaghetti! Yu-mmm." She stretched both arms above her head. "And this time I won't make such a mess eating it."

The next afternoon Trish headed for the barn as soon as she'd changed clothes. She dug carrots out of her pocket and fed each horse down the line, only spending a minute or two with each, until she reached Spitfire's stall where he was cross-tied and already saddled.

"Hello, fella, looks like you're ready to go." She smoothed his forelock and scratched his cheek.

"Dan'l and I already galloped him a couple of rounds to take the edge off him. He's gotten real used to being led around the track." David joined her in the stall. "Are you sure you should be doing this?"

Trish just shook her head. Another worrier.

After the first lap at a walk, she loosed the reins enough to let Spitfire jog the next round. Two new unpainted boards in the fence replaced those she'd broken in her accident, making it easy to tell where she'd gone airborne.

"What a bummer," she said as she stroked Spitfire's neck. "If I *never* do something like that again, it'll be too soon." Spitfire's ears flicked back and forth, listening to her voice and checking out everything around them. "I don't know which is better, the shower yesterday or riding today."

Spitfire snorted.

"Yeah, you're right. This is better."

———

"No, it's too soon!" Marge slammed her hand down on the kitchen counter a week later. "Your arm isn't strong enough for you to race yet. Trish, this time I won't back down."

"But, Mom!"

"No. I don't care what you say. The answer is no!"

"Dad?"

Hal shook his head. "I'm afraid your mother's right."

"But other jockeys get back up with casts and braces and all kinds of things."

"It's different if you have to earn your living riding. You take more chances that way." Hal shrugged.

"But that's not the case here." Marge crossed her arms. "Give it at least another week."

"That's the day I ride for Bob Diego, on the mare he's taking to Santa Anita. I *have* to do that!"

"Okay."

Hal stroked his chin. "Think I'll put Gatesby in the third race that day. That'll give you two mounts and that's plenty for your first day back. Working everybody here will give you enough exercise in the meantime."

Gatesby was up to his usual tricks when they loaded him in the trailer on Friday night. He flipped David's baseball cap off his head and snorted with the first thud of his hooves on the ramp.

"Life is never dull with you around, is it?" Trish kept one hand on the horse's halter as David tied the knot and tugged it tight.

"Get over, horse." David slapped the bay's shoulder. Gatesby had swung his weight so David was pinned against the side of the trailer. He pushed and thumped him again before Gatesby moved over. The horse turned, looked over his shoulder and nickered at Trish and David as they left the trailer.

"Same to you, you stubborn, ornery, hunk of . . ."

"Now, David." Trish swallowed her giggle. "Remember what Dad says. Patience is a virtue."

"Yeah, patience."

Trish slid the bolt home after they raised the tailgate. She'd had a few names for Gatesby herself when her arm was casted.

Real, honest-to-goodness sun brightened the windy March day as Trish bagged her silks and packed her sports bag. Yellow daffodils lined the walk, nodding and bowing her out to the car. Caesar yipped and frisked around her, acting like a puppy on the loose.

"You have everything?" Marge asked as she slid into the passenger's side.

Hal grinned over his shoulder at Trish. "Of course she does. Portland Meadows, here we come. Tricia Evanston is back!"

And being back felt like a huge hunk of heaven. Trish couldn't stop grinning. She laughed when Gatesby tried to nip David in the saddling paddock and beamed at Brad when he took the lead rope. Flags snapped in the breeze and Mt. Hood speared the eastern sky. Gatesby pranced for the surging crowd. He arched his neck, ears pricked forward. He was ready to run.

"You'll do great!" Brad gave Trish the thumbs-up sign when he passed the lead over to the handler at the gate.

The field of eight entered the starting gate easily. Trish gathered her reins. A few butterflies flipped around in her midsection, reminding her that they were still resident.

The gates swung open and Gatesby hesitated enough to put them a half a length behind the others. Trish kept him on the outside, giving him time to hit his stride.

"Okay, fella." She loosened the reins and leaned forward. "Let's make up for lost time." Gatesby stretched out. One by one he passed the field now strung out going into the turn. He pulled even with the third-place runner, then the second as they came down the home stretch.

The jockey on the gray in front went to the whip as they thundered down the last furlongs.

Gatesby pulled even with the horse's shoulder, then they were neck and neck.

"Go, Gatesby!" Trish shouted.

One more giant thrust and Gatesby pushed ahead to win by a nose.

"I think you just know how to stick your nose out straighter," Trish said as she let him slow for the turn back to the winner's circle. "You almost blew that one, you know."

Gatesby tossed his head and jigged sideways.

"Good job, Trish," John Anderson shook her hand and patted her shoulder. "I didn't think you were going to pull it off that time."

"I had my doubts, too." Trish kept an eye on Gatesby's nose as they posed for the picture. "Watch it, Dad!"

Hal flinched away just in time. "You . . ."

"There aren't enough names to call him," David muttered as he clamped his hand on the reins. "Come on, horse."

Trish felt wonderful to be back in the locker room changing her silks. The familiar steamy liniment smell, someone singing in the shower, friendly greetings and 'welcome backs,' all combined to make her good mood even better.

She stroked the mare's neck after Bob Diego gave her a leg up in the saddling paddock.

"You know how Marybegood runs," Bob said. "She's really ready and this is a good field for her. I think you should win it."

"We'll do our best." Trish patted the mare's bright sorrel neck again. "Won't we, girl?"

Trish let Marybegood run easily in third place after a clean break from the gates. With a half a mile to go, she moved up into second and encouraged the mare to stretch out after they rounded the turn. Within two lengths they caught and passed the leader.

Suddenly Marybegood stumbled.

Trish caught herself, one foot out of the stirrup and her left arm clamped around the mare's neck.

At the same time, she tried to keep the mare's head up so they wouldn't go down and be trampled by the hind runners.

Marybegood refused to put any weight on her right hind leg. As soon as the last horse passed them, Trish vaulted to the ground.

"Easy, girl, help'll be here soon." She ran her hand down the leg where swelling had already started.

The horse ambulance pulled up beside them.

"I think it's broken," she told them, hardly able to keep the tears from her voice.

CHAPTER 13

"I'm so sorry, Bob," Trish said for the third time.

"Trish, look at me." Bob Diego grasped her chin between his thumb and forefinger. "This break is not your fault. There was nothing you could do; these things just happen."

"Maybe if I'd . . ."

"No." Hal placed a firm hand on her shoulder. "You couldn't have done anything differently. You stayed aboard and kept her from going down."

"Will you have to put her down?" Trish bit her lip.

"I think not. The vet can pin it and while she won't race again, she'll be an excellent brood mare."

Trish breathed a sigh of relief. "Good. I'll see you after I change, Dad." She turned back. "Where's Mom?"

"In the car." Hal raised his eyebrows.

And not very happy, I'll bet, the thought flitted through her mind.

Hal waited for Trish outside the dressing room. "Bob offered us his horse van for the trip to Santa Anita," he said as soon as Trish met him. "But we'll have a lot of talking to do to make this work."

Trish nodded. "I know."

Conversation never had a chance at life when they

got to the car. It didn't take a genius to tell a storm was coming.

Marge whirled on them as soon as they entered the house. "How many times have I said that racing is just plain dangerous? Today it was the horse that got hurt, but you could have been injured again. Hasn't all you've been through taught you anything?" She paced back and forth, her arm slicing the air as she spoke.

Trish glanced at her father and understood his signal. She kept her mouth closed. If only she could have shut down her brain, too. Her thoughts whirled like leaves caught in a feisty fall wind.

You're not being fair. I wasn't hurt this time. You can't keep me safe by preventing me from racing. Mom, quit worrying!

Hal stepped in front of Marge to stop her pacing. He put his arm around her and Marge dropped her head on his shoulder.

Trish huddled in the corner of the sofa.

"It's okay." Hal rubbed Marge's back and brushed the hair back from her face. "That was scary for all of us, but Trish did a good job out there. She's an excellent rider, you know that."

Trish went over to the recliner for the box of tissue and handed it to her mother. "Come on, Mom. Maybe it was all those guardian angels that kept me from falling."

"Somebody sure did." Hal led Marge to the sofa and sat her down, then sat beside her.

"I don't want you to go to California," Marge stated flatly after blowing her nose.

"I know." Hal nodded. "But let's talk about that later."

Much later, Trish finished the thought. *And I don't*

even want to be around for it.

On the Thursday program, Trish had only one other mount besides Firefly. This would be the filly's last race before Santa Anita. A drizzle blew in veils across the track as the filly danced her way to the starting gate. She broke clean and ran easily, holding the lead until about three quarters of the way around the track.

Trish felt Firefly falter.

Another horse caught them, driving hard on the outside.

Firefly strained forward, throwing herself across the finish line.

"And that's a photo finish, ladies and gentlemen," the announcer's voice boomed over the PA system.

Firefly seemed to be walking gingerly. Trish cut short any extra circling and stripped off her saddle outside the winner's circle.

"Something's wrong." She stooped to run her hands down the filly's front legs. They were already hot.

"All I can say, girl, is you got heart," Trish murmured to Firefly as they posed for the picture.

"I think she won that by a whisker," Hal said. "I'll meet you down at the barn, David."

Trish took a show with her next mount. As soon as she could get away, she trotted across the infield to the back lot.

"It's shins again," Hal answered her question as they met in the filly's stall. "I'm afraid that does it for her this season."

Another Santa Anita scratch, Trish thought. *Are we caught in a string of bad luck, or what?*

She dreaded the Sunday night family meeting that week. And it wasn't because of her grades. The big discussion would be Santa Anita.

In church that morning her prayer was simple. *Make my mom let us go. Help her to stop worrying so much. Please, please, please!*

Trish spent most of the afternoon on her homework so the evening would be free. She set the table without being asked and volunteered to make the salad.

Marge gave her a one-raised-eyebrow look and shook her head.

Trish caught the edge of a smile as her mother turned to stir the gravy. She tried to think of something to say while they worked together in the kitchen, but everything seemed forced or fake. Like, *You know, Mom, how would you like to go to Santa Anita with us?* Or, *How do you feel about your sick husband and young daughter driving that huge van all the way down I–5 to southern California?* But Trish already knew the answers.

Dinner was quiet. Trish finally pushed her half-eaten roast beef and mashed potatoes to the side.

"You feel okay?" Marge glanced from Trish's face to her plate and back.

"I'm fine."

Sure you are, her nagger chuckled in her ear. *Your stomach is doing flip-flops and your hands are shaking. But you're just fine!*

"Why don't we have dessert later?" Hal shoved his plate toward the center of the table so he could prop his elbows in front of him. "No, leave the plates." He laid a restraining hand on Marge's arm as she started to rise.

He cleared his throat. "Okay, let's begin the discussion. David, I'd like to hear from you first."

"I think we should go for it. Brad and I can handle things here while you and Trish are gone. We don't have

any of our horses racing that week so it should be easy."
He smiled an apology at his mother.

"Trish?"

"I won't miss much school 'cause that's spring-break
week. If we don't go, we don't have much of a chance for
the Kentucky Derby and who knows when we'll have a
three-year-old as good as Spitfire again? I think he—we
deserve the chance."

"Marge?"

Marge took a deep breath. "I know all your arguments. I know this race is important to Runnin' On Farm
as a business. I know how strong you are and how
quickly you can get sick." She grasped Hal's hand.
"Mostly I know how terrified I am that something terrible will happen. Every scene imaginable has played
itself over and over in my head."

Hal covered her hands with his.

She continued, "And I know that the only thing holding you back is your concern for my feelings." She looked
around the table, holding the gaze of each for a few in-
tense seconds. "So I say, when do you leave?"

Trish leaped from her chair, slamming it back to the
floor in her exuberance. She threw her arms around her
mother. "All right, Mom! You won't be sorry, I just know
you won't."

Marge hugged her daughter back. "I'm probably already sorry, but let's get on with the planning."

Trish picked her chair up and sank onto it. *We're
going! Please God, with no more hold-ups. We're going to
Santa Anita!*

"Thank you, dear. And I had all my arguments so
carefully planned out." Hal smiled at her.

"Way to go, Mom." David patted her arm. "You and

I can hold down the fort just fine."

"The way I see it," Hal continued after taking a deep breath and letting it all out, "is that we'll leave early Saturday morning and stop in Yreka that night. We'll drive to Adam Finley's farm at Harrisburg on Sunday and stay over there to give Spitfire a rest. Tuesday we'll drive on down to Arcadia. That way we can walk him Wednesday to get him and Trish used to the track, breeze him Thursday and jog Friday. Then Saturday's the race. We'll start home Sunday morning, be back here by Monday night. What do you think?"

"All right!" Trish bounced on her chair.

"Well, *I* think we better get some motel reservations made and make sure you have all you need." Marge counted the days on her fingers. "We only have five days to get ready. Trish, how many mounts do you have this week?"

"Two Thursday and one Friday. Looks like I'll cancel the one for Saturday."

"Good enough. Anything else?" Hal looked at each one of them. "Then what's for dessert?"

"Thank you, thank you, thank you," was all Trish could say that night in her prayers.

————

The week took wings and flew off before anyone could catch it. On Wednesday Hal brought the horse van home and took Trish out for a driving lesson. He taught her about the extra gears with a floor shift and double-clutching to make down-shifting smoother. They drove high in the hills above Hockinson where Hal had her stop and start again in the middle of a steep grade.

"I've always said you were a natural driver." Hal patted Trish's knee as her shifting became smoother and her ear tuned to the sounds of the engine. "I think we better find you a good pillow though so you can relax. Even with the seat all the way forward, you're straining a bit."

"Need longer legs," Trish said as she turned the van back into their driveway. "But I like driving this rig."

"Hopefully you won't have to," Hal pocketed the key when she turned off the ignition. "But we're prepared, just in case."

They loaded the van, all but the horse, on Friday night. Hal had slept in the afternoon and been coughing at dinner, but he assured everyone it was just a tickle in his throat.

"Don't worry," he said. "I've packed extra lozenges and even antibiotics if I need them. Really, I'm fine."

Trish could see worry lines deepen on her mother's brow, but Marge didn't give voice to her fears this time.

Trish was afraid she'd have a hard time going to sleep that night, but she conked out right after her head hit the pillow. The next sound she heard was her alarm. It felt like she'd just fallen asleep.

"Breakfast's ready," Marge called as Trish gave her hair a last brush through. She tugged her rust sweater in place and winked at the smiling face in the mirror. *On to Santa Anita!*

There was a knock on the front door just as she headed for the table. It was Brad and Rhonda.

"We had to see you off." Rhonda threw her arms around Trish. "Oh I wish I were going too."

"Pull up your chairs," Hal said from his place at the head of the table. "You're just in time."

Marge flipped more bacon in the pan. "You can start

with your juice. Two eggs for you, Brad? Rhonda?"

"We didn't come for breakfast." Rhonda hesitated for just a moment.

"Have you eaten yet?" Hal asked. At the shake of her head, he added, "Then sit down. You know you're always welcome here."

An hour later they were loaded and ready to roll. Spitfire, blanketed and legs wrapped, walked up into the van like a pro. Trish hugged her mom, then David, Rhonda and Brad. "You guys are something else. Thanks for coming. And Mom, I'll call you tonight as soon as we stop." Trish's send-off was her mother blowing kisses in spite of her tears, and the other three with their fists raised for victory.

"Eight-thirty, not bad," Hal said as he wheeled the van out on to the county road. "Once we get on the freeway, how about pouring me a cup of coffee?"

The sky was overcast but the rain held off while they drove down the Willamette Valley to Eugene. Trish and her father talked about all kinds of things: her school, gossip at the track, raising and training thoroughbreds. But by noon, Trish could tell her father didn't feel well. His cough became more frequent and he rubbed his forehead repeatedly.

They stopped in Roseburg for lunch and gas.

"You're looking a bit gray around the edges," Trish said when she sat opposite him in the booth at the restaurant.

"Feeling a bit gray, too." Hal rubbed his head again. "All I need is a bug now. Well, I've taken some stuff that should help. What do you want for lunch?"

Trish watched him carefully while she ate her BLT. After he paid the check, she asked, "Do you want me to drive?"

"No, I'll be okay. The break helped."

They opened the rear door of the van to check on Spitfire. He stood drowsing in the deep straw.

"You sure look peaceful," Trish said. "See you later."

By the time they reached Grant's Pass, Hal admitted to needing a break. They stopped at a rest area beside the freeway and after a visit to the restrooms and a walk around to loosen up, Trish took over the driving. Hal propped a pillow behind his head and immediately fell asleep.

Trish hummed to herself as she drove along about 60. She felt herself part of the parade of semis carrying their cargo toward the southland. When she left Ashland, she glanced at her watch. They should make Yreka easily by six o'clock.

She joined the semi-rigs as they shifted down on the snaking four-lane highway up toward the California border and the Siskiyou Pass. Wisps of fog obscured the forest-clad peaks and filled the valleys. As they climbed, the fog closed in on the highway and she had to turn on the lights.

Trish glanced over at her father. *Should I wake him up and let him know what's happening?* She shook her head. *No, he needs to rest so we can keep going.*

A few miles later, just after the check station south of the California border, a fog curtain dropped across the highway. All she could see were the red taillights of the rig in front of her.

CHAPTER 14

"What do I do now?" Trish whispered.

Possibilities chased each other through her mind. She could pull over and wake her father up. *No, he needs to sleep. If he hasn't wakened by now, he must be sicker than he said.*

She could give in to the tears of fear and frustration that pricked at her eyelids. *No, if I'm having a hard time seeing now, what would it be like through tears?*

She could pray. *I'm already doing that!*

She could do just what she was doing—follow the taillights in front of her. When it came right down to it, that was the only avenue as far as she could see—she smiled grimly to herself—which wasn't very far.

Father, I sure need your help now. Please take care of us.

As the miles slowly passed, Trish had no idea where they were. She was concentrating so hard on the road that she missed seeing the signs, shrouded as they were in the soupy fog. She blinked repeatedly because squinting to see made her eyelids tired—and ache.

Fear slipped in the window and pinched her shoulders. It snaked down and stirred up the butterflies roosting in her stomach. Fear wrapped around her hands and bonded them to the steering wheel.

Trish swallowed hard. Her throat felt dry. She needed a drink of water, but she didn't dare take her eyes from the road to reach for the water bottle.

God, help me!

Singing helps. For a change her nagger was being helpful.

Trish began with "Eagle's Wings" and followed it with every song she'd learned in Sunday school, Bible camp and youth group. She sang "Jesus Loves Me" and all the verses to "Michael, Row the Boat Ashore."

As her mind tried to remember the words to all the songs, her hands kept the truck on the road, still following those wonderful taillights.

She sang Bible verses and when she ran out of ones she knew, she sang her favorites over again.

When fear raised its ugly head, she shoved it down again with the name of Jesus. Just repeating His name kept her chin from quivering.

Trish wanted to check the time but couldn't take her hands from the wheel to turn on the light. *How much farther, God? Shouldn't we have been there long ago?*

But there was no place to turn off and she didn't dare lose those taillights.

If the truck pulls off, I'll stop and ask him where we are. Having a plan of action helped. She picked up where she'd left off on "Jacob's Ladder."

The trucker flashed his turn signal for a right exit. Trish did the same. She glanced up just in time to see Yreka on a sign and missed the rest. They stopped at a stop sign and she could vaguely see the word motel outlined in large letters up ahead. When she pulled up in front of it, she read the sign: Traveler's Rest.

"Where are we?" Hal raised himself upright and

peered out the window. "Good, Tee. You found the right place. Did you have any trouble?" He stared out the side window. "How long has the fog been this bad?"

"Forever." Trish leaned her forehead on her hands still clutching the top of the steering wheel.

"Why didn't you wake me?"

"I figured if you were sleeping that hard, you must need it. So I followed some trucker's taillights. He turned off here. Do you think God uses truckers as guardian angels?"

"I'm sure He does, Tee. I'm sure He does."

Trish turned on the interior light. "Nine. Why do I feel like it's about one in the morning?"

"Could be four hours of the most miserable driving conditions in the world. You hungry?"

"Starved." She reached for the water bottle. After a long drink, she wiped her mouth on the back of her hand. "Boy, I needed that."

"Why don't you feed Spitfire while I go in and check on our room?" Hal stepped down from the truck. "Do you have any idea where that trucker went?"

"He's parked at the edge of the parking lot."

Trish watched her father cross the asphalt. The fog glistened in the lights of the motel. She could barely see the truck.

Carefully she flexed her fingers. Her arms ached from clenching the muscles for so long. She opened the door and stepped down. Spitfire nickered. She heard him moving about.

"Okay, fella. I'll get you some dinner, then it's my turn." She stuck a flashlight in her rear pocket, measured grain and separated a couple leaves of hay from the bale. When she opened the people entrance on the side of the van, Spitfire greeted her both with a head in her chest and the soft whufflings that barely moved his nostrils.

"Hey, I only need three hands, now get back, you big goof." She put the hay down and pulled the flashlight from her pocket. By its beam, she set the bucket in the manger and dumped the hay in the sling. A quick flash showed her an empty water bucket.

Spitfire needed attention more than feed. Only when she'd rubbed his face, scratched his ears, and stroked his neck, did she finally shove him toward the feed. He reluctantly left her to begin his dinner.

"I'll get you some water." He left the feed bucket and followed her to the door. "No, now get back. You'll get out after you've eaten."

"We're right in front," Hal said, meeting Trish after she'd filled Spitfire's water bucket. "Number 106." His cough sounded as if it were painful.

"Did you tell that trucker that he was a guardian angel?"

"Yeah. He said that was the first time anyone had *ever* called him an angel—of any kind. But he was glad he could help. Says he drives this freeway every other day but even he gets confused in the fog."

"Why don't I run over and get us some hamburgers?" Trish pulled her small bag from behind the seat. "And you get out of this cold, damp air."

"Okay." He handed her some money.

"You want anything special?"

"A chocolate shake?"

"Now, how come I'm not surprised?" Trish gave him her bag. "I'll be right back."

Hal was already asleep on one of the beds when she returned with two sacks of food.

"Dad, come on, you gotta eat." Trish shook him gently.

Hal rubbed his eyes and pulled himself up against the headboard of the bed. "Thanks. I can't get over how sleepy I am. Must be that medication I'm taking. While it helps clear my head, it puts me right out."

After they ate, they went back outside and lowered the ramp. Spitfire clattered down the ramp, eyes rolling and ears pricked forward. He danced in a circle around Trish, snorting at the truck, the fog, the shadows, anything that caught his attention.

"You want me to take a lead, too?" Hal asked.

"No, you get inside. We'll be fine. He'll settle down pretty quick." Trish clucked to Spitfire and the two of them trotted off around the parking lot. When Trish started to puff, she pulled him down to a walk.

"I'm not used to the altitude," she told him. "And besides that, I haven't done any running for a long time." Spitfire nodded his agreement. Before long he walked with his head drooping over her shoulder.

"I can't carry you and me, too." Trish pushed him away. "So let's get you to bed."

Spitfire snorted and back-pedaled as soon as his front feet struck the metal ramp. "Oh, no you don't." She led him around in a tight circle and this time, he walked right in. Trish gave him a last hug and shut and locked the door. When she tried to slide the ramp back on its rollers, it was too heavy.

"Now what?" She studied the ramp. As soon as the thought hit, she spun and headed for the office. "Could you please help me?" she asked the man at the desk. "I can't get the ramp up and Dad's already asleep."

"Be glad to." He followed her outside and together

they slid the ramp home. "You sure were lucky to make it this far in that fog."

"Yeah, thanks to that trucker." Trish pointed across the parking lot. "He turned out to be my guardian angel tonight."

"Oh. Well—ah—good night then."

Trish shrugged and raised her eyebrows. *Maybe he doesn't believe in guardian angels*. But she sure did.

Hal had left her a note. "I called home. Said we hit a little fog. Sleep well."

No problem there.

It was still foggy in the morning, but after feeding Spitfire, cleaning out the manure, and trotting around the parking lot a few times, they got themselves some breakfast and back on the road. Hal drove, nowhere near as slowly as the night before, until they reached Redding and the end of the fog.

Trish took over the wheel there. It wasn't long before the sun beating on the windshield made her roll down the window. After a morning Coke break, she took off her sweater and let the warm sun shine on her bare arm, resting on the door.

Hal slept some more, and when he woke pointed out the rice fields, the almond and walnut orchards. They stopped for lunch outside of Sacramento, the state capitol.

"We aren't too far from Adam's now, only a couple of hours. No need to take Spitfire out." Hal swung down from the truck cab. "But make sure he has water."

The van was plenty warm so Trish opened all the vents and removed the horse's blanket. Spitfire shook hard, making the whole van shudder. She refilled the water and left him with a last pat. The colt whinnied as if being deserted.

Trish laughed as she joined her father. "Feel that sun? I just know I'm gonna get a tan. Everyone'll be jealous. Ha!"

"Just don't get burned. You're not used to summer sun yet."

"Am I ever? You know what they say about us Washingtonians: We don't tan, we rust."

Trish couldn't believe her eyes when her father drove into his friend's horse farm. "Has this guy got bucks or what?" She stared at the Spanish architecture. The house, the barns all looked like pictures she'd seen of haciendas in old Mexico, with white stucco walls and red tile roofs. Blooming scarlet roses lined all the boundary fences. She could see mares and foals in one section and what looked like yearlings in another. The paddocks seemed to go on to the horizon.

A pair of huge rottweilers announced the truck's arrival.

"Don't worry about them, my friend." The smile on their host's face was about as wide as the man was tall. He'd obviously been a jockey at one time but now had gained a bit in the girth. "Hal, I can't believe it's really you. How many years has it been?"

"Too many." Hal shook the proffered hand. "Adam, this is my daughter, Trish. Trish, after all the stories you've heard about him, you finally get to meet Adam Finley."

Trish felt her hand taken over by the warm grasp of her father's friend. His blue eyes twinkled, as if the leprechauns of his homeland lived inside.

"Let's be getting that horse of yours settled, and then I'm sure you'll appreciate the cold drinks my wife has ready up at the house. And Trish, in case you'd be interested, we have a swimming pool out to the back."

Trish looked at her father, her eyes wide, and shook her head. *I could learn to like this,* she thought.

Trish led Spitfire down the ramp and around an open area a few times before leading him into a roomy stall, apart from the other occupied stalls.

"I'm thinking all your hard work has paid off." Adam nodded his head. He scratched Spitfire's cheek, ran his hands over the sleek shoulder and down the colt's legs. "And you say he goes as good as he looks?"

"He does."

"Well now, and I sure am looking forward to seeing that race on Saturday."

"You'll come all the way down there to see us run?" Trish couldn't keep the amazement from her voice.

"Wouldn't miss it." Adam tucked her hand in the crook of his arm and led them toward the sprawling house. "Now let's go get those drinks I promised you."

The next 36 hours passed like a dream. Trish could have listened to Adam and her father swap stories all night, but finally she went to bed.

After walking Spitfire around the three-quarter mile dirt track a couple of times, then turning him loose in a grassy paddock, she spent the rest of the morning lying by the pool. And playing in the pool. And most of all, lapping up the sunshine. She *did* take heed and slather on the sunscreen. Her dad was right, she couldn't afford a bad burn right now.

When the time came to leave she felt like she'd known Adam and his wife Martha all her life. "Maybe they'd like to adopt me as a grandkid," she said to her father as they drove out the driveway on Tuesday morning. "What a place! And what horses!" She sighed. "I sure would love to ride for him sometime."

"You never know." Hal smiled at her. "I have a feeling that someday you'll have your pick of any mount, at any track."

"You really think so?"

Hal nodded.

Trish re-ran every moment of their visit as they drove on south. What a treat it had been.

Oil derricks at Bakersfield looked like giant grasshoppers nodding above the land. She couldn't get enough of the palm trees, and when they took time for lunch, the riot of flowers around the restaurant stopped her in her tracks.

"Mom would love those," she said. "What are they?"

"Don't ask me." Hal shook his head as he held the door open for her.

He laughed at her awe when they drove the Grape Vine on their approach to Los Angeles. Freeways in every direction blew her away.

"Now watch for the signs for Pasadena," Hal told her. "I have to keep my eyes on the traffic."

"I'm sure glad you're driving and not me."

The Pasadena freeway wound up through rough hills, covered with bushes but no trees. A yellow-gray haze hung in the valleys and blurred the mountain tops.

"That's good old LA smog," Hal said in answer to her question. "Some days are clear and others are—well others are downright awful."

They passed exit signs for Pasadena and Trish saw one for the Rosebowl.

"Now watch for Arcadia and the Baldwin Avenue exit. There should be a sign for Santa Anita Park."

"There it is!" Trish exclaimed a few minutes later. As

they left the freeway they wound through a beautifully wooded area.

"This used to be all one estate," Hal said. "But now this area is a well-known arboretum and park. See, there are the stables off to our left."

Trish sat with her mouth open as they rounded the street into acres of parking lots. The grandstand soared green and enticing above the palm trees ahead and to the right.

"This place is—is," she turned to stare at her father. "It's humongous!"

"Baby, you ain't seen nothin' yet."

CHAPTER 15

"Brian Sweeney's stables?" Hal asked the gate guard.

"Straight ahead, number 26, third barn on your right." The uniform-clad man pointed up a dirt road with low-roofed green barns butting against it. As they drove up the road, Trish could look down lanes leading to the track or deep-sanded walking areas that separated each long barn.

"This is beautiful," Trish whispered, trying to see everything at once.

Since they arrived in the late afternoon, the day's program was nearly over. A couple of horses were being led toward the grandstand. As they stopped the van at barn 26, they heard the roar of the stands. Another race had just begun.

Trish felt like a little country mouse come to the big city. Obviously, horse racing was on a different plane here than up in Portland.

"Brian, how are you?" Her dad shook hands with a dark-haired man who wore a ready smile. She could hear a British accent in the return greeting.

Spitfire nickered as he heard their voices. The van shifted as the colt moved around.

"Brian, my daughter Trish."

"Good to meet you." Brian shook her hand. "Welcome

to Santa Anita. Let's get your horse unloaded so you can move the van. We've a stall all ready for him." The two men pulled out the ramp and opened the back door.

Trish took a lead shank and met Spitfire at the door. He stared out, ears pricked forward. Sun glinted off his blue-black hide. He whinnied, announcing to the world that he had arrived.

Horses answered from stalls around them. Spitfire tossed his head. Trish laughed as she snapped the rope to his halter.

"You're a show-off, you know that?"

Spitfire blew in her face and followed her down the ramp.

"Looks like he traveled well," Brian said. "Why don't you take him to that ring there and walk him for a while, Trish. Loosen him up a bit." He pointed to an oval area between the barns, deeply sanded and with a groove worn by horse hooves.

"You want some help?" Hal asked her.

Trish shook her head. "I need the exercise as bad as he does. Come on, fella. You can check out the sights as we walk."

About half an hour later, Trish led Spitfire down the aisle between the stalls. Each barn was four stalls plus two aisles wide. The aisles had been raked earlier and the cool dimness felt good after the walk. It felt more like a summer day in Portland than early April.

Deep straw bedded the dirt stall. A sling of hay hung on the open upper door and green webbing took the place of the lower door half. Spitfire inspected everything, drank from the bucket in the corner and came back to stand by Trish to get his scratching. She obliged, all the while listening to her father and Brian catch up on the years since they'd seen each other.

I never knew he had so many friends in other places,
Trish thought as she stroked Spitfire's head and neck.

"Let's feed him now, Tee, and then we can get settled
at the motel."

"You needn't worry about a thing in the morning,"
Brian said. "My men will take care of him until you come
to work him out on the track. We have to be done with
morning works by 9:15, so you have plenty of time. Take
it easy, you've had a long trip."

Trish thought back to the fog. *And you don't know the
half of it.*

"We're going to stay here?" Trish looked up at the
bell in the Spanish tower of the Embassy Suites Hotel.
Her father smiled.

"All right!" She gawked even more when they walked
through the inner courtyard on the way to their room.
Lush greenery surrounded a waterfall and running
creek. Brick walks, benches and white-clothed tables
were scattered throughout the airy, two-story room.

Laughing children played around an outside swimming pool, shaded by stucco and brick courtyard walls.
Trish knew where she wanted to spend part of her day.

"I can't believe all this," she told her mother that
evening after she and Hal had dinner in the dining room.
"Oh, I wish you and David were here, too."

In the morning they ate breakfast at the buffet in the
courtyard and headed back to the track.

"That parking lot is bigger than our whole farm,"
Trish pointed out.

"And that's only one of several. Santa Anita has quite
an interesting history. You should go on one of the guided
tours; you'd learn a lot." This time they parked by other
trucks outside the gate.

Spitfire announced his pleasure at Trish's return as soon as he heard her greeting Brian.

"He's already been groomed," Brian said. "We probably should clip him this afternoon. Looks pretty shaggy compared to our horses down here."

Trish tightened the cinch on her saddle. *Yep, they did things differently in California.* Once mounted she followed the two men past lines of barns and out to the huge track.

"Just walk him," her father said. "We'll be up getting a cup of coffee." He pointed to an open restaurant area to the right.

It was a good thing Spitfire was behaving because Trish had a hard time concentrating on him. Off to her left, across a palm tree-dotted infield, the San Gabriel Mountains seemed to butt right against the track. A turf track and another dirt working track also circled the infield.

The stands to her right seemed to go on forever and clear up to the sky.

Spitfire didn't manage a flatfooted walk. He jigged and pulled at the bit. He snorted and reached out to join those horses slow-galloping or breezing by them. Trish got a better look at the stands from the far side of the track.

"There's gonna be an awful lot of people here on Saturday. We've got a big race to run." The enormity of it all dried her throat right up.

By the time Brian took them on a tour of the facility, Trish was even more thunderstruck.

"This area is designed after the English paddocks," Brian said as he pointed out over a landscaped area that looked more like a park than a racetrack. Two sculptures of horses were carved out of bushes. He called them to-piary. "They do a lot of that kind of thing in Europe. And that's Sea Biscuit over there under the awning."

Trish saw a bronze, nearly lifesize statue of a horse on a pedestal. White-clothed tables surrounded the statue.

"They entertain special groups there, serve fancy lunches and programs." Brian led them through the sad-dling stalls and showed Trish the women's dressing area and where to weigh-in in the men's dressing room. "We'll bring Spitfire out and lead him through all this a couple of times during the other races. That way nothing will surprise him."

Or me, Trish thought. *This is all so much more com-plicated than at home.*

She and her father registered that afternoon for their licenses as trainer and jockey in the state of California. They stood in line in the Racing Secretary's office under the grandstand and paid their fees, including the final $6,000 race fee.

"One thing about California, everything costs more." Hal shook his head as he put his checkbook back in his pocket. "Well, come on. Let's go get that horse of ours clipped."

The foreman was just finishing as they arrived back at the stables. "Good horse here." His smile flashed bright against the tan of his face. He, like most of the grooms and stable boys, was of Mexican or South Amer-ican descent.

Trish was tempted to try her Spanish but chickened out. She'd been able to pick up some of the conversations but they all talked so fast. She ran her hand over Spit-fire's shoulder. While the hair was short now, it still had the fuzzy feel of heavier winter coating.

"I'm not used to someone else doing all the work like this," she said as she and Hal walked down the aisles to the track. "But it's nice. David would love it here, don't you think?"

Hal smiled at her. "Let's watch a couple of races, then head back to the hotel."

"Fine with me. You still don't feel good, do you?"

"Not great, but better."

At least the race is the same everywhere, Trish thought as they watched a field break from the gates. After the horses swept by, she looked up behind them to the cantilevered roof of the stands, five stories above them. Crowds thronged both the grandstands and the infield, where there were betting windows, food stands, and a children's play area. *Better keep my mind on the horses.*

Trish fell asleep stretched out on a lounger by the pool. When she awoke in the shade, the first thing she thought of was sunburn. She felt her neck and the backs of her knees and let out a sigh of relief.

"Dad woulda killed me," she muttered as she gathered her towel and slipped her sandals back on. "Hope he's ready for dinner 'cause I'm starved."

———

Back at the track the next morning, she trotted Spitfire through the gap and onto the track.

"Take two laps at a slow gallop, then let him out at that pole," Hal pointed to one of the furlong markers. "We'll clock him at three-eighths of a mile."

Trish did as her father said. Spitfire seemed to have understood the instructions too, at least the part about running that day. But he wanted speed from the very start.

By the time she'd fought him twice around, Trish could feel her right arm beginning to ache. "Go for it!" she hollered as they passed the designated furlong post.

Spitfire didn't need any further urging. He flattened out in three strides, reaching his sprinting speed in a couple of seconds. Trish crouched high over his withers, her face blurred by his mane. After the third post she pulled him down gradually, then continued around the track, slowing to a canter, then jog.

"I know, that wasn't long enough," she sat back in her saddle and stroked his neck. "But Saturday is almost here and then you get to show 'em what you can do."

At the mention of Saturday, Trish's butterflies took a couple of test leaps. She met her father and Brian at the gap.

"We've got the post breakfast in half an hour, so you better hustle," Hal smiled up at her.

"I think he likes running here," Trish said. "Maybe it's the sunshine."

"Whatever it is, he's ready. Stopwatches were clicking around us, so the word will be out right away about 'that Oregon horse.' "

"Da-ad, we're from Washington."

"I know that and you know that but since he's only raced at Portland Meadows, that's where his times will come from."

"Oh." Trish licked her lips. She had so much to learn.

At the breakfast, she felt about as welcome as a toothache. It was easy to see who the jockeys were and there wasn't another female among them.

"This is put on specially for the owners, trainers and jockeys," Brian was saying.

Trish looked around the room again. She stopped and looked back. Sure enough. She pulled on her father's jacket sleeve.

"Dad, that's Shoemaker, isn't it?" She nodded at a gray-haired, jockey-sized man across the room.

"Sure is," Hal answered.

"Would you like to meet him?" Brian smiled at her. "He retired here at the track and has gone into training. Come on."

When Shoemaker shook her hand, Trish's "Pleased to meet you" came out in a stutter.

"Good luck in your race tomorrow," the great man said. "You have a mighty strong field out there."

"It includes one of yours, doesn't it?" Hal asked.

"That's why I can't wish you too much luck," Shoemaker smiled as he spoke. As another person asked him a question, Trish stepped back and watched.

How she would love to hear some of *his* stories, of horses he'd ridden, of races won and lost. He'd been injured more times than anyone cared to count, but he went on to become one of the winningest jockeys in racing history.

Number seven became their post position at the ceremony during breakfast.

Nothing else seemed important after that.

Until they started schooling Spitfire that afternoon. Following Sweeney's instructions, Hal led the colt over to the receiving barn where a farrier checked the colt's shoes. From there they entered the line of saddling stalls where horses for the next race were being saddled. Spitfire danced some when he was led around where the spectators could look him over.

Trish walked beside the colt, talking to him, explaining what was happening and how he should behave.

"I think you must talk horse," Brian teased her when she led Spitfire back into one of the open stalls. They stood there for a while, giving Spitfire all the time he needed to become comfortable.

The next stage was the walking paddock where the jockeys mounted and again spectators could view the entrants. Spitfire walked around the circular railed area with the other horses. When the bars opened for the mounted animals to proceed to the track, Spitfire watched them leave.

Trish watched the majority of the crowd stream back into the grandstand to prepare for viewing the race. "Something to see, isn't it fella?" She looked up on the grandstand where stylized tan horses adorned the forest green siding. A flashing light board announced the odds on the horses running.

Around them, sculptured ancient olive trees offered shade to those sitting on the benches. A circular fountain, surrounded by stunning bright flowers, spouted water in a perfect arc.

"You know you're racing where some of the greats have been, don't you?" Trish said. Spitfire rubbed his forehead on her shoulder. "John Henry ran here, and Sea Biscuit. Aren't you impressed?" Spitfire shook his head and acted bored.

"I think he's seen enough," Hal leaned over the rail. "Let's leave it until tomorrow."

Friday followed much the same pattern. By now Spitfire acted like he'd always raced at Santa Anita.

That afternoon Trish took some time in the gift shop by the front gate to buy sweatshirts for David, Rhonda and Brad. She couldn't decide what to get her mother.

There were T-shirts and hats, pictures and jewelry. Even jackets, all with signs and slogans about Santa Anita. Finally she chose a T-shirt with a picture of a mare and her foal on it. "Mother Love" was the caption.

Sure wish you were all here, Trish thought as she paid for her purchases. *I need all of you to tease me out of my willies.*

When she called home that night there was no answer.

"That's funny," she said, turning to her father.

"What is?"

"They're still not home. I've tried a couple of times."

"They must have gone to a movie." Hal switched off his light. "How are you feeling?"

"Scared spitless."

"Well, spitting isn't polite anyway."

Trish threw one of her pillows at him. "You know what I mean."

"All you have to do is give it the best you can. If God wants you to win, you will. That's why you don't have to be afraid."

"But all those people. And if we don't win, we won't go to the Kentucky Derby."

"True, but that's part of this business. You win or you don't win, but you go for the glory anyway because you love racing. It gets in your blood."

"But Dad, I want to win so-o bad."

"So do I, Tee. So do I."

Trish snuggled down under her covers. *Please, Heavenly Father, help me do my best tomorrow.* The roar of the crowd filled her ears as she finally drifted off to sleep.

CHAPTER 16

Trish found a card propped against the lampstand in the morning. "I can do all things through Christ who strengthens me." Phil. 4:13. Trish read it through several times.

"Thanks, Dad." She slid into the seat across from him in the dining room. "I needed reminding."

"We all do." Hal sipped his coffee.

"Now if we can just convince my butterflies . . ."

Spitfire trotted out on the track for his morning workout like he owned the world. Ears pricked, neck arched, he surveyed his kingdom and found it to his liking.

Trish breathed in the cool, crisp air. Bits of cloud still hovered on the mountains, but the sun was quickly drying dew that sparkled on the grass of the turf track. The weather report was for low 80's with a slight breeze.

"No rain down our necks today, fella." Trish rubbed his neck along the high poll. "Nice fast track. Who could ask for anything more?"

I can, Trish thought later, after Spitfire was polished to the nth degree. Even his hooves shone. *I wish David were here. And Brad on Dan'l to lead us to the starting gate. And Rhonda screaming for us.*

"I even miss Mom telling me to be careful," she said to Hal as they walked out to the truck to get her silks and their racing saddle. "Can you believe that?"

When the crowd roared at the start of the first race, Trish's butterflies flipped and flopped. *Sure is easier when I have several mounts*, she thought. *Then I don't have so much time to stew.*

Worried are you? her nagger's voice accused.

No. Trish tightened her lips. *Scared stiff!*

"What's causing the tight chin?" Hal asked as he handed her a Diet Coke.

"All those other jockeys. Some of them are world-class. They've been racing for years."

"So?"

She cocked her head to the side. "So, Spitfire and me, we're gonna show them that Washington horses are every bit as good as they are." She nodded her head. *If I say it often enough, maybe I'll begin to believe it.*

When Hal and Brian led Spitfire off to the receiving barn, Trish followed and walked around to the women's dressing room. Contrary to the bustling scene in the dressing room at home, she had this one all to herself. There were lockers, a sofa in front of a TV, and even a lighted make-up mirror; but nobody singing in the shower, no one wise-cracking about the last race.

She dressed, locked her things in one of the lockers and left the quiet room.

Brian knocked on the door to the men's dressing room for her. "Woman coming in!" he hollered to alert the jockeys.

Trish clutched her saddle to her chest and stepped on the scale, carefully keeping her eyes down. *Talk about humiliating!* She could feel the red creeping from her neck all the way to her forehead.

"That's 122," the steward said, after slipping ten

pounds of lead into her saddle pad. "Good luck."

Trish fled the room.

The field of ten were all present in the stalls, along with a couple of schoolers. Trish handed her saddle to Brian Sweeney and walked a round with Spitfire. When he nudged her arm, she rubbed his neck.

Back in the stall, Brian squatted down to check a leg wrapping. Spitfire flipped the man's hat off.

"Up to your old tricks, are you?" Hal asked the horse.

Trish fetched the hat. "Sorry, it's kind of a game with him. Guess you can feel part of the family now."

Brian brushed the sand off the tan brim. "Thanks, old man. I needed that."

Spitfire tossed his head. Trish could tell he was laughing.

Hal tightened the over-cinch on the racing saddle just before the number-one horse led the way to the walking paddock. They hung back a bit because the horse in front of them was skittish.

Suddenly a woman screamed as the thoroughbred's hind feet struck for the stars, throwing clods of dirt over the crowd along the railings.

"Never a dull moment," Brian smiled, shaking his head. The horse in front of them acted like nothing had happened and walked on ahead.

After Spitfire snorted his way around the paddock once, Brian held the colt while Hal gave Trish a leg up. She settled her feet in the stirrups and looked down at her father.

He patted her knee. "You know what to do. I'm proud of you."

Trish swallowed. One of her butterflies flipped a cartwheel while another commanded order.

"Trish! Trish!"

She looked out over the crowds. Who could be calling her name?

Then she zeroed in on a leaping figure, arms waving above a bright-red head. Trish stared in disbelief. "It's Rhonda! And Mom! And David! Dad, they came!" She felt like jumping from her horse and charging out to meet them. "They came! They really came! Hey, you guys!" Trish waved her hand above her head, not jockey protocol or cool, but who cared at this point?

Rhonda pushed through the crowd to lean over the rail, and the others followed. "We were scared to death we wouldn't make it in time."

"Would have been here an hour ago except some idiot had an accident and tied up the freeway." David reached over to pat Trish's knee. "How're you two doing?"

"Great! Mom—I—all of you . . ." Trish blinked away the sting in her eyes. "I can't believe it! You all came!"

Marge had to blink too. "We decided we just *had* to be here. And we wanted to surprise you, Trish."

"That you did!" Hal smiled and turned to Brian. "I'd like you to meet the rest of my family." He introduced Marge and David and then Rhonda.

"You'd better get in line," Brian said after greeting everyone. "It's time."

"Go for the glory, Trish!" Rhonda gave her the thumbs-up sign.

Trish swallowed hard and grinned at them all. "Thanks." Hal led her up the padded walk to the cavern through the grandstand where riders waited to lead them to the post.

Trish heard the bugle blast. A woman rider on a gray peeled away from her spot by the wall and took the lead shank. They broke out of the shade and onto the track.

The sun glinted sparks off Spitfire's shiny hide. The saddle blanket with a number seven flapped in the breeze. The riders led them past the grandstand and on around to the far side of the track.

Trish forgot the crowds. She forgot the famous jockeys. She concentrated on Spitfire—and began to relax.

The blue and white starting gates were moved in position about even with the gap, and she and the other entrants trotted forward.

"If you win this, you'll be the first woman to win the Santa Anita Derby," her rider said. "So go for it!" She handed the lead over to the official in slot seven.

Trish waited for the number six horse to settle down before she entered the gate. After their assistant unsnapped the lead shank, Spitfire looked straight ahead. He settled himself, ready for the shot.

Trish crouched tight over his shoulders.

And they were off!

Spitfire broke clean. He ran easily, head out, ears tracking those around him. By the quarter-mile post, the field had separated and Spitfire was running with the front four.

"Come on, baby," Trish encouraged him with her musical patter. "Let's move on up."

Spitfire lengthened his stride. As they went into the far turn, the four appeared to run neck and neck. Coming out of the turn and entering the stretch, a bay made a bid for the lead.

"Now, Spitfire!" Trish gave him his head.

One horse dropped back. They eased up on the second place. Passed that one and headed for the leader.

Trish used her hands and voice to cheer him on.

The other jockey went to the whip. Spitfire caught him at the mile marker. The two ran stride for stride, thundering down to the wire.

Spitfire eased ahead.

The other horse pulled even.

Spitfire reached again, each stride demanding the lead. They won by a head.

Trish rose in her stirrups to bring him back down. "You did it! We did it!"

She turned and cantered him back to the flower-box-bordered winner's circle. She slid to the ground and fell into her father's arms as David grasped the reins. Trish tried to stop the tears streaming from her eyes but that was no more possible than controlling the grin that split her face.

"We did it! We did it!"

When they led Spitfire in front of the risers, Marge and Rhonda joined them on the second tier. Hal accepted the trophy and Trish wrapped the floral blanket given to jockeys over her shoulders. Flashbulbs popped, and Brian led Spitfire off to the receiving barn for the mandatory testing.

"How does it feel?" A reporter stuck a mike in front of Trish's face.

"Fantastic! One of these days I'll come back to earth—but not too soon." Trish linked arms with her mother and father.

"Are you planning on the first Saturday in May?"

"Are we ever! Kentucky get ready!"

"Do you know how much you won?" Rhonda asked her as they walked back under the grandstand. The dim tunnel was the entrance for the race horses.

"Two hundred and seventy-five thousand dollars!"

Trish grabbed Rhonda's arm. "I can't even count that far."

"I'm just thankful you're safe," Marge admitted, hugging Trish again. "I get so scared and so excited at the same time. I think I beat David's arm to death."

David rubbed his bicep. "I think so too. She was jumping and screaming as bad as Rhonda was on my other side. They both used me for a pounding board."

Trish smoothed her hand over the flowers across her shoulders. "Wish this would last. We gotta get lots of pictures. Hey, all of us were in the picture! We won't have any."

"Don't worry," Hal said. "I'll get them from the track. They always give copies of the official pictures to the owner, breeder, trainer and jockey. That should give us a few."

"Congratulations Hal, Trish." Adam Finley stepped in front of them. "My girl, you rode like a veteran on that one." He shook her hand, then gave her a hug. "Hal, you've got some rider here."

Trish tucked his words in the back of her mind to ponder later. Praise from a man like Finley was something to cherish.

Brian Sweeney added his congratulations when they got back to the barn. "You handled him well, Trish. You and the colt are a good team, even if he is a bit of a clown."

Trish told David what had happened in the saddling stalls.

"So he got you, too?" David shook his head. "Usually I'm the brunt of his clowning, but at least he doesn't bite. Not like another horse I know."

"Gatesby," Rhonda and Trish said at the same time.

"I wish Brad could have come too," Trish said as she looked around their group.

"Somebody had to stay home and do chores," David said.

"And I wanted our whole family together for this." Marge linked her arm with Hal's.

"That's the bad part of farming," Hal added. "Someone has to be there to do the chores."

Later that night they gathered in the dining room at the hotel. Hurricane lamps flickered on white-clothed tables. Heavy, wrought-iron chandeliers and wall sconces lit the beamed ceilings.

After a dinner that left everyone groaning from overindulgence, Rhonda asked Hal, "Have *you* ever been to the Kentucky Derby, Mr. Evanston?"

"No, almost made it once—as a spectator—but something happened and I didn't go. I've never had a horse this good before."

"It'll be *some* trip then." Rhonda's eyes widened at the thought.

"Sure will. And we'll be flying there." Hal smiled at Trish. "No fog that way."

"Fog? You told me on the phone it was a problem. But is there more you didn't happen to mention, Hal?" Marge wondered.

"Not really, Mom. But there'll be no fog this time. Only eagle's wings." Trish giggled at the look of confusion on Rhonda's face. "You know our song, don't you?"

Rhonda nodded.

"Well, the airline's called *Eagle Transport*, so it looks like we'll be flying on eagle's wings after all!"

Hal nodded. "Haven't we always?"

ACKNOWLEDGMENTS

My thanks to Brian Sweeney, thoroughbred trainer/owner at Santa Anita, who so willingly shared his time, expertise, and love of racing with me. Thanks also to Director of Communications, Jane Goldstein, and staff for assisting me in my research at Santa Anita.

Gordon Tallman, Public Relations Director at Portland Meadows, has been an ongoing, invaluable aid with his knowledge and enthusiasm for the sport.

Friends of writers never know what they'll be called on to do. Barbara Rader learned more than she ever dreamed she wanted to know about horse racing in our two days of research at Santa Anita. Thanks for being caring and curious. We had fun.

Thank you to Ruby MacDonald, friend, fellow-writer, and critiquer and to husband Wayne who is always game for new adventures.

And finally, Editor Sharon Madison and the Bethany House staff make me feel like someone special. Thanks, folks.